her spy to hold

book two, spy games series

PAULA
ALTENBURG

This book is a work of fiction. The characters, incidents, and dialogue are drawn from the author's imagination and are not real. Any resemble to actual events or persons, living or dead, is entirely coincidental.

Published by Paula Altenburg
Stewiacke, Nova Scotia Canada
B0N 2J0

Copyright © 2016 by Paula Altenburg
Cover design by Syd Gill/Syd Gill Designs
Interior formatting by Author E.M.S.
Edited by Nancy Cassidy/The Red Pen Coach

ISBN: 978-0-9937166-2-1
www.paulaaltenburg.com

Printed in the U.S.A.

He bent his head and pressed his lips to the corner of her mouth, offering a soft, gentle caress. A breath of a sigh—a tiny exhalation of air—brushed his cheek in response. She shifted ever so slightly, whether by accident or design he couldn't be sure, but either way, her mouth glided beneath his until full contact was made. She tugged on his lower lip, the tip of her tongue stroking against it.

Fireworks exploded inside his brain. He'd meant to come across as nonthreatening. To let her set the pace. Dr. Glasov, however, could kiss.

She was as attracted to him as he was to her. Of that much he was certain. While the timing wasn't the best, and he'd never coax her into doing anything she might regret in the morning, he wasn't about to pass up an opportunity he might regret missing either. But they each needed to be clear on what they were willing to offer. There had to be boundaries.

ACKNOWLEDGMENTS

I'd like to thank Author E.M.S. for their formatting expertise; Syd Gill of Syd Gill Design for the beautiful cover; and Nancy Cassidy of The Red Pen Coach for her editing skills.

And of course, a special thanks to Annette Gallant for being my first reader and a great friend.

CHAPTER ONE

"I'VE HAD A BREACH in security at work. I need to speak with someone from CSIS."

The indifference of the Royal Canadian Mounted Police officer lounging in the chair across the table from Irina Glasov was a roadblock she hadn't anticipated. To her, it was simple. The Canadian Security Intelligence Service handled espionage. She was working on a top secret project she wasn't at liberty to discuss with a police detective who didn't have the proper clearances. In order to speak to CSIS anonymously, however, the RCMP would have to contact them for her and arrange a meeting.

Those were the facts.

She laced her fingers together in her lap. She was a thirty-two-year old computer applications software engineer who held two masters degrees and a doctorate in computer science. She designed weapons systems placement for military aircraft. When she spoke in her field, people *listened*. Surely, she could make this one police officer take her seriously. But she'd never been in this type of situation before. She didn't know what else to do. How she could explain it any better, when she found it so puzzling herself.

"I don't understand why you can't report it through your workplace. They must have their own security management measures in place," the detective replied.

Irina tried one more time. "The company's security management measures are inadequate for a breach of this nature. The project I'm working on is top secret. I report directly to the client. No one else in the company has my level of government clearance."

Detective Buchanan glanced at the clock on the wall. "Miss Glasov. Let—"

"Doctor," Irina interrupted.

A gray-speckled eyebrow went up. Calloused fingertips stroked the laminate tabletop. "*Dr.* Glasov. Let your client know they have a problem. Let them contact CSIS. We don't report every little thing we hear. There are also privacy issues to be taken into consideration. CSIS gathers intelligence and distributes it to worldwide organizations. That's why we screen the leads we hand them. If this is someone at work having a bit of fun with you, you don't want to bring CSIS down on them."

Having personal photos pop up on her computer monitor—through a secure intranet system—wasn't a "little thing" or someone having a "bit of fun," and she doubted that CSIS would want to share this particular piece of intelligence with other organizations. The end customer for her work was most likely a foreign government, using a third-party broker to buy work from her employer.

But she couldn't tell him any of that. While she had no idea how many similar requests Detective Buchanan handled in the course of a year, it was safe to assume very few. Enfield, Nova Scotia wasn't exactly a hotbed of international terrorist activity.

He wasn't going to do anything for her. Coming here had been a waste of her lunch hour. She stood, smoothing the wrinkles from her navy pencil skirt, and extended her hand. She'd already given him her contact information, although she didn't expect him to use it.

"Thank you for your time," she said.

She had no idea where she should turn now.

Kale Martin rarely got tired of tailing stupid people. They were an endless source of entertainment.

Two men in expensive suits walked into Durty Nelly's, an Irish pub on the corner of Argyle and Sackville streets in downtown Halifax, for the third time in a week. By Kale's count, this was meeting number seven. It was as if they were daring CSIS to tag them.

Suit one, the investment banker, liked to play extreme sports. He got his kicks off the thrill of danger. He probably thought this was some kind of game. But his companion…

The second man wore a suit well. He was polished. An excellent spin doctor. No doubt about that. He and his entourage also had terrorist links all the way from ISIL to an up-and-coming little sect currently stockpiling an arsenal in a small, North African nation. Even the local Hell's Angels chapter steered clear of these bad boys. Extreme Sports Investment Banker was in way over his head.

Kale didn't have a whole lot of sympathy. It was the money trail that interested him the most about this little duo, and he'd found the connection. Now he was intent on figuring out what would make the banker guy squirm.

What would scare the crap out of him enough to make him squeal like a little girl on a playground who'd had her hair pulled. And he'd already decided it wouldn't take much more than an unannounced, but no less official, visit from CSIS to the banker's place of business. Rule number one of organized crime—don't shit where you eat.

"Are you ready to order?"

Kale looked up from his glass of soda to find the pretty blond barmaid who'd been eyeballing him all week standing beside his table. Most of the other women in the pub weren't above staring at him, but it seemed clothes really did make the man. The courier uniform and short pants he wore kept their interest from progressing beyond the eyeballing stage.

The outfit didn't appear to be a turnoff in this case, however. He smiled at the girl as he passed her the menu. She had the fresh-faced look of a college girl, young and sweet. He was a sucker for sweet.

Young, not so much.

"I'll have the salmon with sweet potato fries," he said.

She smiled back, clutching the menu he'd handed her to her chest, in no hurry to leave. "You must be new on your route. You're turning into a regular here."

Kale had a general fondness for women. They liked him too, although he rarely acted on what they offered. He moved from city to city, and country to country, with a frequency that wasn't exactly conducive to long-term relationships. He wasn't a big fan of the associated break-up drama, either.

Still, a little flirting never hurt anyone. He broadened his grin, showing off the thousands of dollars his parents had invested in orthodontics when he was a kid. "If all the girls here are as pretty as you, I'll be a regular for sure."

She blushed. "If you need anything, ask for Mandy."

"I will, indeed."

Kale ate his lunch when it arrived. The two men he was watching had ordered drinks to go with their steaks, then another round for desert. They looked like they were settling in for the afternoon.

He couldn't sit here that long. Even the extreme sports banker guy would get wise to that. He glanced at his watch. He'd hired on with the courier company so he'd have a reason to be in the downtown area every day, but his immediate supervisor knew nothing about his job with CSIS. He didn't mind being fired—this particular assignment was over anyway—but it didn't sit well to know that people were waiting for business deliveries that might be important. They had their work to do too.

He left the money for his meal, along with a generous tip, on the table. He'd parked the delivery van in a loading zone out front, its four-way flashers blinking. One of the perks of being an intelligence officer for CSIS. No parking violation tickets in the city would stick as long as he wasn't blatantly blocking traffic.

As he got in the van, he saw the second man—the scary one—come out of the pub, look up and down the street, and spot him.

He jogged over.

Kale cranked down the window and stuck his head out to greet him, resigned. This was going to be ugly. "Can I help you with something?" he asked. "Got a delivery you'd like me to make?" It never hurt to try.

He saw the fist coming at him but didn't have time to dodge it completely. He shifted his face to the left so it missed his nose, connecting with his cheekbone and eye socket instead. The side of his forehead, right above the temple, slammed into the edge of the van's open window frame. Pain, white-hot and blinding, exploded through his whole head.

Turned out it did hurt to try, after all.

When Kale's vision cleared the guy was still standing there, shaking his fingers.

"I don't know who you're working for," the other man said in a low, pleasant voice, "but I'll take a guess. The next time you bastards want to follow me, try remembering that I've got rights to privacy in this country and a whole team of lawyers. Asshole."

Once he'd delivered his message and that last parting shot, he walked back to the pub as if nothing had happened.

That had gone better than expected. Kale touched his fingertips to his tender, swelling cheek and winced. It was mid-August on a sunny afternoon in downtown Halifax. There was no way the incident had gone unobserved. A small crowd had already begun to gather on the sidewalk.

A man rushed up to the van. "Are you OK? Want me to call the cops?"

Kale waved him off, signaling that he was fine. This wasn't the first time he'd been punched and it wouldn't be the last. It beat getting shot. "Thanks, but no worries. The guy's upset because I slept with his wife. I had it coming."

That last part was true. He really did have it coming. He'd been as careless and stupid as the investment banker he'd been tailing. It wasn't a complete loss, however. CSIS already had the information it needed.

His cell phone rang. He reached into his pocket to retrieve it. "Hello?"

"Kale Martin? This is Detective Dave Buchanan from the RCMP detachment in Enfield. Your office gave me your number. I was wondering if you could maybe make a stop out here sometime this afternoon."

Irina was cooking dinner when the knock came on her kitchen door.

She froze with the steel knife she'd been using to chop green onions for an omelet suspended in midair. She wasn't expecting visitors.

She laid the knife on the wooden cutting block, then crossed the kitchen to the two-panel steel side door of her bungalow, the one that led to her carport, and peered through the curtain.

Thor stood on her doorstep, hulking and blond, and scary.

He wore his hair in a man bun. The wide smile on his lips and the ridiculous courier uniform did nothing to offset the alarming effect of the shiny black eye and the hint of a bruise on his forehead.

There was no need to overreact. All of her doors and windows were locked. The air conditioning took care of the summer heat and humidity.

She left the chain in place on the inner door, opening it only far enough so she could speak through the crack. The locked exterior screen door added another layer of protection. It wouldn't stop him if he tried to force his way in, but it would slow him down enough for her to slam the inner door shut and shoot the deadbolt.

"You must have the wrong address," she said. "I'm not expecting a delivery."

"Dr. Irina Glasov? My name is Kale Martin. Detective Buchanan suggested I pay you a visit. He said you'd asked for a meeting." He fumbled in his shirt pocket for a piece of ID. He flipped it open and held it up.

She couldn't get a close enough look at it through the screen, not that it mattered. She'd never be able to confirm the legitimacy of it even if she did. Hope warred with suspicion. "Do you mind waiting a few minutes while I give Detective Buchanan a call to confirm who you are?"

The giant didn't take offense to her caution. "Not at all."

She left him on the doorstep while she dug her cell phone and the business card Detective Buchanan had given her out of her purse. She punched in the number.

As it turned out, the detective had, indeed, asked Mr. Martin to stop by. The description he gave her matched the man at the door, right down to the black eye, courier uniform, and running shoes, but Irina continued to hesitate even after she disconnected the call. The pop-ups had been unnerving and she was cautious by nature.

She wished she were taller and more assertive. A self-defense course wouldn't have been remiss either. She took a deep breath. She was a woman living alone who'd had a bad day. She'd let Mr. Martin in, but she'd stand at the counter so she'd have the knife close at hand. She'd never be able to use it on anyone, but he didn't need to know that.

She slid back the chain and unlocked the screen door. She didn't open it but retreated to the counter, leaving him to let himself in.

The Norse god stepped over the threshold, his sheer size swallowing what she'd considered a spacious kitchen. If he lifted his hand above his head he could plant his palm on the ceiling. Fine gold hairs sprinkled tanned calves and forearms. Bulging biceps and broad pectoral muscles strained the seams of the gray cotton, short-sleeved shirt. Faint blond scruff, caught in the light from the bay window, stubbled his jaw.

The guy was beautiful. She had a difficult time believing he was an intelligence officer. Weren't they supposed to blend in?

The only place he'd go unnoticed was Asgard.

His blue eyes, sparkling with geniality despite the bruise and the swelling, took in the knife on the counter, but if he had an opinion about it, he kept it to himself. Instead, with a discreet deference for her nervousness, he moved to the table in front of the window, putting some distance between them.

"Do you mind if I sit?" he asked, pulling out one of the round-backed pine chairs.

She'd prefer it if he did. He had to be close to a foot and a half taller than her underwhelming five feet, two inches. Factor in her boring brown hair and he made her feel like a Hobbit. "Help yourself. Do you mind if I ask how you got the black eye?"

He touched his cheekbone and made a wry face. "Funny story. True story. Turns out not everyone likes couriers. Who'd have guessed we could be so offensive?"

The bruise looked painful. And fresh. She couldn't begin to imagine who would have the arrogant confidence to punch a man his size in the face. Nor did she wish to.

Her sympathy was hard to suppress, however, especially since she was the reason he was sitting here, rather than at home, where he'd no doubt prefer to be at the end of a rough day. "Would you like ice for the swelling?"

"I would *love* some."

The refrigerator stood to Irina's left, closer to her than

to him, but if she moved, it meant being out of reach of the knife. He might be gorgeous, but she wasn't stupid.

He saw her split second of indecision and gave her an out. "I can get it myself." He pried himself from the chair. As he opened the freezer door, she took note that his glutes weren't bad either. He got additional points for his polite consideration. He pulled out a small bag of frozen peas and held them up, shooting her an inquiring glance over his shoulder. "Can I use these instead?"

Irina found her tongue. "Go ahead."

He reclaimed his chair, propping an elbow on the table and pressing the bag to his face with a sigh of pure bliss. "Thanks. That feels a lot better." He fixed her with his good eye. "Detective Buchanan tells me you work for a defense contractor, doing something with computers."

His tone was unreadable. Still, she could imagine what he must be thinking. What he saw. She hadn't been expecting this visit, not after her meeting with the detective, so she wasn't at all prepared. She'd ditched her office attire for denim shorts and a clingy pink tank top that made her look young. Her lipstick was long gone. At least she'd left her hair up, secured in a semi-professional, loose knot on top of her head, even though it was likely a mess. It was where she kept pencils for scribbling down notes and equations.

"Yes and no." She wasn't giving up too much information just yet. "I work through the defense contractor, not for them. They won a contract to build a specialized unmanned aerial patrol vehicle. A drone. They hired me to work with them to enhance it."

"What do you mean by 'enhance'?"

"This is the part where I have to ask how high your security clearance is," she said.

He removed the bag of peas and stared at her, slack-jawed. "Specialized patrol drone... My God. You're designing weapons. For a *Canadian* contract?"

Irina understood his reaction. Canada prided itself on being a nation of peacekeepers, not peacemakers. Officially, its military patrol aircraft weren't armed. Instead, they were designed with the capabilities for armament. It was a technicality, but a significant one. While Canadian contractors weren't under any obligation to work only with Canada, there were laws restricting what countries they could supply weapons systems to. Stringent ones.

"So you see why I need to know what your security level is," she pressed him.

"It's high enough for the basics. For now, you can keep the details and any names to yourself."

His honesty impressed her. He didn't try to pretend that his clearance was better than hers. And he was willing to hear her out. Relief left her shaking. She had to lean against the counter behind her for support. For the first time all day, she felt safe.

He rubbed a finger along his upper lip as he continued piecing the details together, thinking out loud. "So your company is building the drones but the customer is arming them."

"I don't know who's arming them. I handle the weapons systems designs—their placement—nothing more. The contractor builds the drones, which are then delivered to the customer. My designs are a separate delivery. For all I know, the customer could be a distributor. A middleman for someone else."

He sprawled in the chair, the sheer size of him making it creak, and settled the bag of peas against his face again.

"You can correct me if you like, but I'm going to make a few assumptions based on what you are—and aren't— telling me. One of them is that these are nuclear weapons we're talking about, and the final customer could well be a foreign country Canada doesn't do business with because they haven't signed the Nuclear Non-proliferation Treaty." He paused. When she said nothing to contradict him, he continued. "Explain to me why you believe you have security issues?"

"This morning, I started getting pop-ups on my computer at work. They were photos of me." She cleared her throat. "Private photos."

He dragged a slow glance from her bare feet to the top of her head. She felt herself blush. So she wasn't porn-star material. *Thanks for noticing.*

"Not that kind of private. Just...private." She waved her hand to encompass the kitchen. "Taken of me here. In my home. Through the windows."

His expression cleared. "That explains why you've drawn all the curtains."

"The photos aren't the real issue." Though they were bad enough to unsettle her. Nobody liked having their personal space invaded. "The problem is with the pop-ups themselves."

"Pop-ups... Aren't they the annoying little ad things that get in the way when you're trying to read articles on the Internet?"

"Yes. They're also a type of spyware that gathers information on the site's users. Some of it's for marketing purposes, like how many click-throughs a user makes on a site. Some pop-ups are more invasive than others."

"I was told you have a PhD in computer science. Can't you clear them off your computer yourself?"

"I did already, but the computer's not mine, it belongs to the company. I work within specific parameters and resolving intranet security issues isn't part of my job. I'm supposed to go to tech support for issues like that. In turn, they're to investigate and report any security breaches to the company. But if I go to tech support, I run the risk of making the problem public and therefore more difficult to resolve. The contractor has a secure intranet system. How did these pop-ups get there? Who else knows about them? And why are they aimed specifically at me? Is anyone else getting them, too?" She hated all the unanswered and inexplicable questions. She liked for things to make sense and this made none at all.

He frowned as he parsed her dilemma. "So if pop-ups are a form of spyware, these could be gathering information on your designs from your computer."

"In theory, yes. But in this particular case, no. Not the designs themselves. All classified work is done on an isolated computer in a locked room. Everything's password-protected. Not even tech support can get into it. There's no intranet or Internet on that computer. That one's secure. External hard drives used for backups are stored in a separate locked storage room that can only be accessed by two people. Everything has to be signed in and out."

"Then if the designs are protected, I'm afraid I really don't see how this is a matter for CSIS."

Her chest tightened. She shouldn't have to connect the dots for him. "Not to toot my own horn, Mr. Martin, but I'm something of a world authority on weapons systems placement design and my brain's not locked in any classified storage area. Since someone is targeting me specifically, I'd think that would be a serious concern."

Thor gave her a slow, heated smile that brought a blush to her toes. "You're also an attractive woman. Maybe you have an admirer." The smile slid from his lips. "A creepy one, granted. Call Detective Buchanan back and tell him about the photos. He can do more for you than I can in terms of personal protection."

Her fingers bit at the edge of the smooth, granite counter. If she were a man he'd never make such a ridiculous assumption. The people she worked with all had high-level security clearances. While that didn't preclude them from stalking, it did mean they weren't stupid enough to jeopardize those clearances for a little titillation. And the average stalker, even with better-than-average computer skills, wouldn't be able to break into an intranet system of this caliber.

She was back to square one. And she no longer felt safe.

CHAPTER TWO

DR. GLASOV WAS CUTE when she was mad—all pokered-up lips and imperious green eyes.

The pink cheeks and that light dusting of freckles on her perky little nose made it impossible for Kale to picture her as a weapons systems design expert. The denim short-shorts and super-revealing tank top didn't help, either. She looked more like an indignant pixie.

Dang, she was pretty.

But there was no doubt she was also scared, and his size and the black eye were currently working against him. She wasn't giving him enough information to work with. Someone at CSIS might have more intel on the situation she'd described.

To him, however, it sounded more like a case for CSEC—Communications Security Establishment Canada. They dealt with cybersecurity. His personal knowledge of computers wouldn't get him a passing grade in a first year programming course. His area of expertise was languages. He was fluent in six and spoke seven Arabic dialects. The best he could do for her was to make a call to his team leader and pass on what little information he had.

At the same time, he couldn't walk out the door and

leave her like this. As far as protection went, that knife on the cutting block beside her was a joke. She'd never be able to use it. It didn't take a PhD in anything to see she'd probably pass out if she tried. How she'd gotten into designing nuclear weapons systems placement, of all things, was a complete mystery.

He tried to soften the blow. "Irina... Can I call you Irina? Because saying 'Dr. Glasov' makes me feel like you're about to examine my prostate or something." She smiled a little as she said yes, just a faint twitch of her lips, and he continued on a more serious note. "I agree that these pop-ups are disturbing, and I do think you should be concerned for your safety. But CSIS gathers information for national security. We aren't law enforcement. You really need to call Detective Buchanan back."

A hint of fear flickered in those pretty green eyes. Guilt punched him in the gut. He'd made matters worse, not better, by confirming what she already knew—she should be afraid and he couldn't help her.

"I'll do that," she said.

She wasn't going to though. Underneath the fear was a layer of stubbornness. He could see it in the lift of her chin and the tightening of her jaw, and the way her whole body went rigid at his recommendation.

Fair enough. It was her decision to make. Besides, he'd had a hard day too. His head ached and his face hurt. It was time to leave. He pushed out of the chair and took a few steps across the kitchen, the bag of frozen peas in his hand.

Her eyes flew wide at the sudden movement. She backed a step closer to the cutting block behind her.

He stopped. He might have been wrong about her ability to use that knife.

But he didn't think so.

He brandished the bag of peas. "I'll put these away before they thaw out. Then I'll be on my way."

She slumped against the counter. Embarrassment flooded her face. Pressing her palm against her chest, she took a few rapid breaths. "Sorry. I guess I'm a little jumpy today."

"Perfectly understandable."

He got it. He really did. She was a woman living alone and he looked like he'd just come from some sort of crazy-assed couriers' rumble. But it bugged him that she thought he might hurt her. He'd been raised to treat women right.

The peas safely back in the freezer, he retreated to the door leading from the kitchen to the carport. He fished a business card out of his pocket. All it had on it was his name and a phone number. He dropped the card into a ceramic dish on a tall pine stand by the door that held a set of car keys and an airport security pass.

"There's a good chance someone's having fun with you," he said. "Mean fun, granted. Maybe it's professional jealousy. Even smart people can do stupid things, particularly if their emotions or pride are involved. But if you think of anything else I can do to help, or if anything new happens, feel free to give me a call."

"Thank you." Her tone said *when hell freezes over*.

He let himself out. Behind him, he heard the chain slide into place and the deadbolt shoot home. Dr. Irina Glasov, supposedly a well-respected expert on nuclear weapons systems placement design and well aware of her worth, was far too scared for him to dismiss this as someone's idea of a joke. There was simply very little he could do for her other than file a report.

He walked from the shade of the carport to his van in

the driveway. The blazing heat of the late afternoon sun beat through the cotton shirt of his uniform. He looked around him with more interest than he had when he arrived.

The neighborhood where she lived was semi-rural, the subdivision made up of properties segmented by acreage and not postage-stamp-sized lots like the ones on the outskirts of the city. Her nearest neighbor's house was well back off the road and hidden by trees. If anyone was watching her, or tried to break into her home, it was doubtful they'd be noticed.

As he backed the van out of her driveway, he decided not to sit on her problem. He'd report it asap and let someone else worry about it.

The city was twenty-five minutes away.

When he got to his apartment he changed into gray board shorts and a black T-shirt, stuck a frozen pizza in the oven, and cracked open a beer. He'd call in sick at the courier office in the morning, then tomorrow afternoon, he'd hand them his resignation. After that he was basically logging time until his next CSIS assignment. He planned to do some kite surfing out at Lawrencetown Beach while he waited.

First though, he had a report to phone in. He sank into the padded leather sofa that faced a 55 inch, HD Smart TV and flicked on his cell, punching in a series of numbers with his thumb. "Dan. Hey."

"Kale. What's up?"

He filled his team leader in on his day, glossing over the part about getting punched in the face. He had his pride. When he got to the part about Irina Glasov, however, Dan had plenty of rapid-fire questions. What defense contractor was she working for? How many people had she told about this? Did her story ring true?

"It does." Kale tried not to think of the fear in her eyes she hadn't been able to hide. If he did, he'd lose sleep. "But from what little she told me, this is more a cybersecurity issue than something for CSIS. CSEC should probably be brought in."

"I'm not so sure about that." Kale lifted his feet off the coffee table and sat up straight at the change of tone in his team leader's voice. "It's like this. We've got a bit of a situation here in Ottawa that I can't really get into right now."

Politics were a few levels above Kale's position and normally, he liked it that way. He focused on deciphering the real message his team leader was trying to deliver. Something about CSIS not sharing information with other organizations or government departments until further notice...

He gripped the phone tighter. "Wait. What was that?"

"It turns out a target another officer has been tracking with regard to missing weapons systems parts has friends in very high places. Therefore, all reports having to do with Canadian defense contractors and weapons systems are to go through the director for vetting until further notice," Dan said. "Nothing gets passed on without his seal of approval."

Friends in very high places took on a more ominous tone. CSIS reported directly to the federal ministers of Public Safety, Justice and Defence. If information wasn't being passed on to other government departments, it meant either the director didn't want the ministers to know about something so that they wouldn't be culpable for it, or he was worried about some sort of leak.

Shit had just gotten real.

It also meant the cute weapons systems placement

designer wasn't going to get any help from CSEC unless the director of CSIS approved sharing the information with them, and her problem was currently overridden by national security concerns.

Kale hung up the phone with a tight knot in his stomach. He tried not to think about Irina, with her green eyes and freckles, messy hair, and the pretty pink tank top she obviously hadn't realized showed off her nipples in such specific detail. She didn't strike him as the sort of woman who flaunted her wares, as his grandma used to say. She didn't seem like the type to overreact either.

And yet, she'd been scared.

He ate his pizza, then prowled around the apartment, restless and in need of a distraction. There was nothing on TV that he wanted to watch. Heading to a bar for the evening was out of the question. There was always some drunken jackass wanting to fight, and a black eye screamed, *"Pick me. Pick me."*

But he was bored. Concerned. And fresh out of distractions.

He could always drive back to Irina's and sit in his car for the night. No one would recognize it. The more he thought about it, the better the idea sounded. There'd be no harm in it.

As he was gathering his car keys, however, his cell rang.

"Here's the deal," Dan said, getting right down to business. "It turns out Dr. Glasov really is working on a project that's of interest to CSIS. The problem is that the director doesn't want anyone to know there's a problem. If you catch my meaning."

He did. "What do you want me to do?"

"It wouldn't hurt for you to keep an eye on Dr. Glasov. Unofficially, for now. We're going to put this on your vacation time and transfer the hours later. That gives you five weeks. There are bigger stakes in this for Canada than the designs she's working on. Mind you," Dan admitted, "those are important too. She's got quite a reputation. *Really* impressive."

The fine hairs on Kale's arms prickled. "Just so we're clear. You want me to spy on her?"

That so wasn't cool. While there were always exceptions, the CSIS Act clearly stated that it only spied on Canadians if a threat of terrorism was somehow involved. Of course, anything involving weapons and weapons systems could be considered a threat. It all depended on how the director planned to spin any reports. Or if he even planned to make them.

"She's not under investigation. We're trying to find out what's going on and how she's connected to it. Why don't we call it 'establishing friendly and mutually beneficial relations' instead?" Dan suggested. "How you approach her is up to you."

Whatever they wanted to call it, it meant Kale could phone Irina first before he camped out in her yard. He felt better about that. She'd feel better knowing CSIS was taking action too. He'd keep the unofficial part of it to himself.

As for what was happening in Ottawa, he'd leave that up to his superiors. He had no interest in politics.

The call from Kale Martin surprised her. Irina hung up the phone, uncertain what to think. What emotion to feel. On one hand she was glad to have a CSIS officer watching her house.

On the other, his presence confirmed she had a real reason to be concerned.

Now that CSIS was involved, however, it was as if a great weight had been lifted from her shoulders. This was no longer solely her problem. Someone else was in charge. So, as far as her choice of emotion, she went with relief. Plus, he'd sounded so reassuring on the phone.

"I don't want you to be alarmed if you notice a strange car in the neighborhood tonight," he'd said. "I drive a blue, four-door Toyota Camry. And I'm going to be following you for a few days, just to find out if anyone else is too." There'd been a brief pause. "I don't suppose you'd make me a pot of coffee?"

The unexpectedness of the request, as well as the little-boy hopefulness in his tone, had broken the last bit of the tension inside her. She wasn't certain if he'd been entirely serious about the coffee or making a joke. All the same, this was her chance to make up for her ridiculous jumpiness around him earlier.

The jumpiness, if she were honest, was only partly thanks to those photos. The rest had to do with him. Although the jury was still out on the link between human pheromones and sexual attraction, the amount of testosterone Kale Martin exuded left her feeling awkward around him. She didn't like the sensation.

She'd already showered and donned her pajamas, and been working on an upcoming presentation for a conference in France when he'd called. She considered getting dressed, then decided it wasn't necessary. He was only coming to the door for a minute, and her bathrobe and slippers were conservative. Nothing said sexy like wet hair and flannel.

She turned on the coffeemaker and rummaged through

the cupboard for a thermos. He'd said he was a half hour away. That gave her time to make sandwiches too.

Thirty minutes later, she watched headlights approach through the trees on the dirt lane leading into the subdivision. The lights slowed at the end of her driveway, continued on past, then a few minutes later, returned. As the car passed beneath a street light, she saw it was a blue, four-door sedan. Whether or not it was a Camry, she couldn't be sure.

The car stopped and pulled over to the shoulder as if parking for the night, well out of range of the patchy street lighting. Based on the angle of the photos she'd seen, he'd chosen a spot farther along the lane from where they would have been taken. She had no idea what happened next, or what to do with the coffee and sandwiches. She'd assumed he would come to the door. Should she take them down to his car instead?

Not a chance. It was dark outside and she hadn't gotten over all of her fear. If he wanted his coffee, he could come and get it himself.

Ten minutes later, just as she was thinking he hadn't been serious and she should go to bed because she had to work in the morning, she heard a soft knock at her kitchen door, followed by a quiet voice.

"Irina? It's Kale. Can you let me in?"

Her heartrate accelerated. It seemed they were now on a first name basis. She checked before opening the door to make sure it really was him, then slid the chain free.

He crowded into her kitchen, forcing her to back up a few steps, and locked the door behind him. He scrubbed at his head with both hands and swatted his clothes. "Wow, the mosquitoes are aggressive tonight. I think I lost a pint of blood walking up your driveway."

She couldn't smother a smile. Despite his size and the bruised face, and the fact he was prettier than she was, his friendly manner was definitely disarming. She could appreciate it more now that she wasn't so panicked.

He'd changed from the courier uniform into board shorts, boat shoes, and a navy sweatshirt, and looked more like a surfer tonight, although the tiny pair of binoculars dangling from the strap around his neck seemed a touch out of place. She still found it difficult to believe he was CSIS, but that was probably the point. If he'd arrived wearing a dark suit and glasses, with wires sticking out of a breast pocket, it might look suspicious.

"Thank you so much for coming. I made sandwiches to go with your coffee," she added, then winced inside. She sounded like his mother. Or a spinster aunt. She had no idea how old he was. At a guess she'd say late twenties, possibly thirty, only a few years younger than her thirty-two.

"So you're smart, beautiful, and a good cook, as well as thoughtful. Did you get all the luck and talent in your family too?" he asked.

Definitely charming.

"I'm an only child. And your assumption that I'm a good cook might be premature."

"You are." He grinned, all confidence. "You have a professional set of knives and a whole lot of kitchen gadgets, including a food processor. One of your sinks is used for prepping vegetables. There's a small-appliance garage in that corner of your cupboard. Your cutting board is made of maple and it's well used. Your freezer is full and everything's labeled and dated. The wooden spoons by the stove are stained. If I didn't already know you're a computer scientist, I'd think you were a professional chef."

She was speechless. He'd noticed a lot when he was here earlier, yet she could have sworn he'd been indifferent to his surroundings and would have preferred to be elsewhere. "I'm impressed."

"I am pretty impressive," he agreed, nodding cheerfully. "Wait until you get to know me better. I'm full of great surprises." He glanced at the neatly wrapped stack of sandwiches on the counter with undisguised lust in his eyes. "Can I have one of those now? Because from here it looks like they're Montreal smoked meat on rye. And if that's gourmet Dijon mustard you used, then I think I'm in love."

His sense of humor, combined with the random shifts in conversation, made her head spin. She wasn't sure what sort of response he expected from her, so she went with the safest. "Your coffee's in a thermos. Did you want to eat here or take everything with you?"

"Yeah. About that..." He cleared his throat. "It's going to look odd for a stranger to be sitting in a car outside your house all night. The neighbors will call the police. I considered hiding in the trees instead, but the mosquitoes have pretty much nixed that idea. I've already made my personal donation to their blood bank on the walk up your driveway. I thought I might set up shop in your living room. If you don't mind, that is." He waggled the binoculars at her. In his massive hand, they looked like a toy. "These are night vision, by the way. Very high tech. We aren't Canada's *numero uno* spy agency for nothing."

This joke, she got. And it was funny. "So that's where

all our tax dollars go—buying you people fancy spy equipment. Do those convert into a telephone too?"

His proud grin was too cute for words. "Even better. These babies can be used as a blunt instrument. Since you work with weapons systems, you should be able to appreciate their versatility. No stealing the idea, though. I'm betting it's patented."

She clutched the neck of her robe. "I'm going to sleep so much better knowing how well protected I am."

In fact, quite the opposite was true. She had reservations about letting him stay. While it would be nice to have another person in the house, this particular man wasn't the best choice. He was easygoing, true enough. He seemed fun as well.

He was also a whole lot of...man.

Irina had earned one of her masters' degrees and her PhD by the time she was twenty-one. That meant in high school and university, she'd been far too young to socialize after hours with her classmates. These days she couldn't remember a conversation with any colleagues that didn't include strings of code, or computer simulations involving hydrodynamic, radiation, and neutronic effects.

Kale didn't look at her the same way they did. She felt a bit like that smoked meat on rye sandwich. She was book smart and people stupid, and so out of her comfort zone right now, she was about to make a complete fool of herself. His being here was part of his job.

Best not forget that.

"So...it's OK if I stay here, then?" he asked.

"Make yourself at home." She reached for the thermos and sandwiches and carried them to the table, then got him a plate and a coffee mug from the cupboard. "I'd stay up and keep you company," she added, "but I have to go to work in the morning."

He picked up a sandwich and unwrapped it. "Understood. I'll follow you to your office when you leave, then head back to the city and get some sleep. I'll meet up with you again around five o'clock in the parking lot. Tomorrow's Friday. You won't be working late, will you?"

The way he phrased the question made it sound as if only losers worked late at the end of the week.

"No," she said. "I have plans."

"Really? Anything good?"

He looked so surprised it was insulting. She had a life.

"I'm having dinner and drinks with a friend. I might spend the night." The friend was a woman, but he didn't need to know that.

"You and your friend won't even notice me," he assured her. "I'll have to stay in the car though. The black eye's a little limiting in public. It draws too much attention." He took a bite of the sandwich and chewed before swallowing. An expression of bliss lit up his face. "Man, this is good."

Her head was spinning again. She hadn't really thought about what it would mean to be followed. The loss of privacy wasn't an issue, but having him discover she didn't have much of a private life to watch was going to be tough on the ego. "I don't want to be any more of an inconvenience than necessary. If it's easier for you, I can stay home."

"That would definitely be easier. But this isn't about me. Carry on as usual."

With a man like Kale Martin following her around?

"I'll see you in the morning," she said, and fled to her bedroom.

She closed the door and leaned against it. Except for work and this latest development, her life was boring. Exceedingly so. Maybe he'd judge her for it, maybe not. Her suspicions leaned toward yes.

How could he not?

CHAPTER THREE

THE DINNER DATE WASN'T a man. At least, not one who was close to her. If she'd had a significant other in her life, he'd be the one spending the night here with her to make sure she was safe.

If Irina were his, he wouldn't be leaving the job to another man. No way in hell.

Kale prowled silently around her house, checking out her belongings, trying to understand what made her tick. For a scientist, she had a definite girly side. Her living room looked like the inside of a dollhouse, all frilly and pink, right down to the matching sofa and loveseat. It was as if a cotton candy machine had exploded in here. He couldn't find any crochet materials, or craft tools of any kind, so he suspected the lace doilies on the coffee and end tables had been a gift from some ancient aunt, or maybe a grandmother.

The bookshelves filling one entire wall were another revelation. Scientific textbooks—dozens of them—dog-eared and battered, were crammed together with books on the occult.

Like that wasn't freaky.

Two thick tomes on computer coding had her name on

the spines. He tugged one off the shelf and flipped through the pages. Intellectually, he was no slouch. He'd graduated near the top of his class. As well as a talent for languages, he had a master's degree in Western studies. But he was an arts major and these books were beyond him. He put the tome back.

She fascinated him.

Frustrated him, too. He'd done his best to be friendly. He'd made a few jokes. He'd complimented her cooking, which hadn't been difficult. Those sandwiches were amazing. Over the protests of his man genes he hadn't stared at her either, exhibiting amazing restraint on his part, because her flannel pajamas and robe hadn't hidden a whole lot. Even though she was on the small side, the woman had curves. She was pretty and smart, definitely out of the ordinary, and he was attracted.

He, on the other hand, scared the hell out of her.

He should leave well enough alone.

He spent the rest of the night alternating between peering from behind the curtains with his binoculars and taking short catnaps on the pink sofa. He didn't mind shiftwork and often worked odd hours, but it always took a few days to acclimatize.

The coffee, while as good as the sandwiches, was no match for his circadian rhythm. He woke to find the sun streaming through the living room windows and Irina hovering in the archway leading to the dining room attached to the kitchen. She was fully dressed and had her car keys in her hand, and was staring at him with an expression of uncertainty on her face as if she couldn't quite make up her mind what to do.

Since she was already dressed and had been staring at him, he didn't feel too bad about taking a slow, visual inventory of her in return. He liked the high heels. They showed off a great pair of legs. The narrow skirt wasn't nearly as prim as she no doubt intended. And she wore a snug white T-shirt under a short-sleeved red jacket that had to be her version of Friday office casual. The thick knot of light brown hair at the back of her head and its stray wisps of curls whispered *sexy*.

Not simply *sexy*. *Sexy as hell*.

Hopefully, he hadn't been talking in his sleep, because he'd been dreaming about her. Naughty things, too.

She was blushing as if she were reading his thoughts. Or, maybe he had been talking in his sleep, after all. He scrubbed a hand across his chin. Stubble scratched at his fingers. "What time is it?"

"A little after seven-thirty. I need to be at the office by eight." She hesitated. "Would you like me to make you breakfast?"

She was like two different people. As Dr. Glasov she might be all prickly about her fancy reputation, but at home, her Irina persona seemed to have missed the whole feminist movement.

Maybe she was just exceedingly polite.

He swung his feet to the floor and sat up. "Thanks, but I'll grab something at home. Let's get you to work. Mind if we use your car? I'll pick you up later."

Her office was fifteen minutes away. He'd hoped to be able to get a sense of her workplace and coworkers, but she worked from one of the hangars at the international airport. It had direct access to the runway, so security was tight. He could get inside if he wanted to because of his government clearances, but since his status on Irina's case was unofficial, he didn't want to try. It would be the equivalent of waving a big red flag with *CSIS* emblazoned across it.

He'd have to be more creative.

The parking lot outside of her building required parking passes for staff use, but if he sat in Irina's car and looked as if he were waiting for her, no one would bother him. That was why he'd asked if he could use it. The commissionaires who acted as security guards in these places tended to notice a lot, but at the same time, weren't uptight vigilantes about it. Unless he gave them a reason to think he was up to no good, they'd leave him alone.

The black eye was going to be a problem however. The swelling was gone but the colors could light up a runway. The commissionaires would definitely notice him and wonder what he was up to. They'd give his description to the Port Authority at the airport terminal. The Port Authority would be able to track him straight back to CSIS in a matter of days, if not hours. The director would lynch him.

That meant he'd continue to use Irina's car, but he had to come up with a plan as to why he was there every day waiting for her.

By midmorning, he had one. And it was a beauty.

When five o'clock rolled around he had her car parked in the fire lane next to her building, the most conspicuous place he could find, watching everyone who came and went. He was more interested in the people entering at the end of the day than the ones who were leaving, but they didn't need to know that. He stared at them all. They all stared back.

At ten after five Irina exited through the main doors, her jacket draped over one arm, the laptop bag hanging from her shoulder and thumping against her hip. She wasn't alone.

The stout, pepper-haired male accompanying her might be older by a good fifteen years, possibly twenty, but Kale had no trouble identifying the guy's interest in her—and it wasn't for her brain. He stood too close as they talked. He made a point of touching her arm. His gaze dropped from her eyes to the twin swells beneath her tight little T-shirt, not so often as to be overt, but often enough.

It was equally obvious that Irina was all about business. Whoever her dinner date was, this wasn't it. Kale sighed. She had no clue. The pop-ups on her computer could very well be coming from someone in her office and she'd never figure out who it was. Not without an electronic trail she could follow.

It was time to put his plan into action.

He opened the car door and got out. He walked over to the main door where she and her companion were talking. She stopped in mid-sentence at the sight of him. The sun caught the surprise in her eyes, highlighting their unusual, pale shade of green.

"Hey, babe," he said. He draped an arm around her shoulders and kissed her. Before she could recover and demand to know what he was up to, he stuck out a hand to the coworker. "Kale Martin. Friend of Irina's." He laid extra emphasis on the word *friend*.

"George O'Brien." He pumped Kale's hand up and down, his grip firm, his round face curious. Disappointment lurked in the flat line of his mouth. Speculation narrowed his eyes. "Irina never mentioned she was seeing someone."

Kale gave her shoulders a squeeze, then released her. "She likes to keep her personal life separate from work. Don't you, babe?"

"Yes. We have that in common."

She sounded more bemused than annoyed. She was smart, quickly determining this was part of his cover—which it was. But not entirely. He'd had no reason to kiss her, or call her babe, other than that he'd enjoyed doing both.

Her colleague wasn't yet ready to call it a day. "So, Mr. Martin. What do you do?"

Kale had answered this particular double-edged question too many times to take any offense. Everyone assumed because he was big, he was dumb. Most days, it suited his purposes.

"I'm a substitute teacher. Kinesiology."

To an academic that translated as an unemployed gym teacher, and O'Brien couldn't hide his condescension. "I would have guessed you were a boxer."

"Because of this, you mean?" Kale touched his eye and laughed. "I got this out at Lawrencetown. I was kite surfing and lost control of my board."

"Kite surfing, huh? Sounds like fun." O'Brien turned to Irina. "I'll see you Monday. Don't forget we have that progress meeting at nine." With a wave of his hand, he moved off.

Once he was out of earshot, Dr. Glasov faced Kale. A stray strand of hair had crept loose of its knot and she tucked it behind one ear. Her eyes had cooled to green, tempered steel. "I have to work with these people. I'd rather not be called 'babe'."

She never mentioned the kiss. He'd have thought that would be the greater transgression. Good to know that it wasn't. "'Dr. Babe' has a nice ring to it," he said, just to mess with her. "Next time I'll give that a try."

The steel in her eyes melted. A grudging smile stretched to her lips, and just like that, she was Irina again.

She was such a fascinating contradiction. As a professional, she had a high opinion of herself. Justifiably so, according to CSIS. But as a woman…

"I sound like a snob, don't I?"

"Little bit. Yeah."

"You took me by surprise. I don't think I've ever been called that before," she confessed.

"What, babe? Or snob?"

Her smile deepened. The sun brought out the faint sprinkle of freckles on her nose. Kale felt a hot jab of pure lust, straight to the groin.

"I'm sure I've been called a snob any number of times."

The heavy glass-and-steel door banged against the concrete wall next to them as someone pushed through. As she moved out of their way, the strap of her laptop bag slid down her arm. He reached out and caught it. The laptop was in no danger of hitting the ground. He simply liked having a reason to touch her.

"Here. Let me carry this for you." He tugged the bag free of the crook of her elbow. She gave it up without protest.

They walked to her car. He unlocked it with a press of the button on the key fob and set the laptop in the backseat. When he straightened, she was standing beside him. Out here in public, where anyone could see them, she wasn't as wary of letting him close. He might as well take advantage of it.

"I need to get an idea of the people you work with," he said. "Even though I have the clearances, it would look suspicious for someone like me to start working in your department all of a sudden. And I'm not good with computers, so it would seem even stranger for me to be hanging around you. A better reason would be if everyone thinks we're a couple."

A touch of pink colored her cheeks. "I figured that out."

"So you'll understand when I do this."

He didn't give her any other warning than that, because Dr. Glasov could poker up fast. Irina however...

Such a contradiction.

He bent his head. Her eyes opened wide, her long lashes fluttering. He slid a hand behind her neck, tilting her chin upward. He kissed her.

This one wasn't a casual greeting. Not even close. The second his lips touched hers, his half-assed plans for establishing a cover story deserted him. Her fingers clutched at his hips, no doubt to steady herself because he'd caught her off guard, the heels of her palms pressing too close to his groin. His body reacted. His free hand found the small of her back and he drew her against him so that she could feel his interest for herself. He ran the tip of his tongue across the seam of her lips, teasing it open. She tasted of cherry. A stroke of the pad of his thumb along the sensitive spot on her throat, beneath her ear, made her gasp. They were both breathless now. He wondered what sounds she'd make if he were inside her, and if he dared to find out.

A helicopter flew low overhead on its flight path to the runway nearby, bringing him back to reality. They were in a parking lot at her place of work. And there was a fine line between establishing that they were couple and being cited for public indecency.

Yes, his thoughts had definitely gone there.

He lifted his head, although he didn't let go of her. He couldn't. Not yet. He scrambled to come up with some explanation for what he'd just done.

She beat him to it.

"That was very convincing." She smoothed his shirtfront and stared at his chest, avoiding his eyes. "But you're wasting your time. There's no one from my office out here to see us, only the commissionaire on duty. And I'm fairly certain he's not paying attention."

Kale could have told her that the commissionaire was the intended audience, and yes, he'd most definitely been paying attention. All he'd really needed to establish was a reason for being here in the mornings and afternoons, when people were coming and going.

Instead, as he opened her car door for her, he said, "Then I guess we'll have to try again Monday, won't we?"

Irina slid into her chair at the Press Gang where her friend Beverley was waiting for her.

By the looks of it, Bev was already a few glasses into the bottle of wine on the table. Irina could use a few drinks herself. It had been that kind of week and the intelligence officer assigned to her wasn't improving it. He was good at his job.

Too good. That kiss had seemed real.

The waiter came over to pour her wine. She thanked him, her fingers trembling ever so slightly as she picked up the glass. Most nights she loved this restaurant. It was quiet and intimate, and the low-beamed room with its dark, polished wood gave a real feel for the history of the city. Halifax was an international sea port—the first European settlement here dating back to 1749—and a former naval stronghold. Irina had grown up on the Canadian prairies, so having the sea so close at hand was a novelty that never grew old.

Tonight, all she wanted was to bury her head under her blankets until this whole mess was behind her. She had no idea who might be watching her or what harm they intended, either to her or her project. And Kale... Well, he'd completely messed with her head. She liked working with numbers and facts, not suspicions. She preferred her world neat and tidy. Her emotions too.

The worst of it was, she couldn't let on to her friend that anything was wrong.

"You look like hell. I'm going to guess that work isn't going as well as it could," Bev said, her smile sympathetic, but she knew better than to ask too many questions. A mathematics professor at Dalhousie University, she was a number of years older than Irina—although Irina couldn't have said how many with any degree of certainty. Her skin was too perfect and she covered the gray in her hair with a platinum rinse. They'd met at a conference in Ottawa and struck up a friendship. Women in the sciences tended to stick together.

While Irina couldn't get into her problems at work, Kale Martin was another matter. If they were going to be in a pretend relationship, then he was fair game when it came to gossiping with her friends. Bev had been married three times. This was one problem she could help with.

It was new conversational territory for them however. Normally when the two women got together, they talked about the challenges of working in academia for Bev and with the military for Irina. She wasn't sure how to approach it.

"I met a man," she blurted out.

Bev looked at her over the rim of her glass. "It's about time. I was beginning to wonder which team you played for. Not that it matters."

"I was starting to wonder about that myself."

She wasn't, of course. She liked men. Her luck, however, hadn't been great. The few men she'd gotten involved with over the years had been even duller than she was, and while she had no craving for excitement, there seemed little point in two people slowly boring each other to death.

But Kale was at the extreme other end of the spectrum.

Being with him was the equivalent of tandem skydiving with a single, shared parachute.

Bev finished her drink. "So tell me about him. How did you meet?"

They'd gone over their story in the car. "Stick close to the truth," he'd warned her. "Don't make it something your mother wouldn't believe."

"We met at the beach. I was reading a book and he was surfing. He couldn't fathom there was a woman alive and breathing who wasn't paying attention to him, so he came over to see what was more fascinating than he was."

Bev laughed. "I bet he got a shock."

"He wasn't the only one." No point in getting so far into this fairy tale that she couldn't escape. "I don't see it going anywhere though. We don't have enough in common. Right now I'm a challenge to him, but sooner or later, the novelty will wear off." That much was true.

"So what if it does?" Her friend dismissed those concerns with a shrug of her slim shoulders. She topped off Irina's drink with the last of the wine and signaled to the waiter to bring them another bottle. "There are plenty more men in the world. Why not have fun while it lasts?" She waved the empty wine bottle at her. "Don't marry him, though. Not unless he earns more than you do. Divorces are expensive."

Irina took a healthy sip of her wine and picked up her menu. Kale was driving and she might as well make the most of it. But if they were going to be drinking, she needed food in her stomach. "I'm fairly certain marriage isn't on either of our minds."

"Then I don't see your problem."

As the evening wore on, Irina no longer saw it either. Kale was hot. He didn't seem to mind kissing her. She wasn't so boring she couldn't figure that out. But they weren't really involved with each other, and nothing good ever came from mixing business with pleasure.

One hour slid into two and she began to feel guilty. Surveillance might be part of his job, but at the same time, she didn't need to be inconsiderate about it. He'd be waiting for her.

"I should really be going," she said, sneaking a glance at her watch. "I was supposed to meet Kale at 8:30." Underneath the sapphire crystal, the numbers were blurry. It looked like they read nine o'clock, but that couldn't be right.

Bev's eyes brightened. "He's picking you up? Can I meet him?"

Irina couldn't see why not.

They paid the bill. Outside, the brightly-lit street was noisy. They were in the middle of the downtown bar district on a Friday night. Cool, salt-scented air flowed off the harbor. Irina tucked her purse under her arm, her jacket in her hand, and looked up the steep street toward the Halifax Citadel. Kale and the car were right where she'd left them, about six parking meters up, on the opposite side of the street.

He must have been watching for her. He got out of the car and started walking toward them. He wore tight jeans and a white cotton shirt, unbuttoned at the throat to expose a few inches of chest. The blond man bun showed off his high cheekbones. If not for the fading black eye, the whole image would have shouted something straight out of *GQ*.

"There he is."

Her friend's eyes widened. "If only I were twenty years younger..." she breathed. "*That* is a whole lot of man. You go for it, girl. You're too smart to be passing that up."

Irina might be smart about some things, but in this particular instance she was so ignorant it hurt. She didn't know how a real relationship worked, let alone a pretend one. She'd also had too much to drink. It might be best if she took her cues from him as far as introductions went. Or anything else, for that matter.

"Hey," he said, stopping in front of them.

"How tall are you?" Bev blurted out, awed.

Kale's lips twitched. "Six five. And I'm guessing you ladies had a few drinks with your dinner." He looked at Irina. Flustered, she dropped her purse. He bent to retrieve it at the same time she did and their foreheads collided. "Maybe more than a few," he murmured to her, sounding amused as he returned her bag. His mouth hovered a few inches from hers. For a second she thought he was going to kiss her again and her heart skipped a beat. Instead he caught her arms and helped her straighten, his blue eyes smoldering with good humor as if he knew what she'd been expecting. "Why don't we drive your friend home and call it a night?"

She rubbed her forehead, which was now on a level with his chest. The intimacy he suggested with his use of the word *we* unsettled her far more than the bump. A little fresh air might be a good idea before she got in the car with him.

"It's still early. Why don't the three of us go for a walk along the waterfront? Or get a coffee somewhere?" she suggested.

From behind Kale's back, Bev made a face at her and mouthed *don't be stupid*. "You two go ahead without me," she said out loud. "I'll call a cab."

Kale's eyes fastened on Irina's. His simmered with heat. "I had a long night last night. I expect another long one tonight. I'm ready to go home." He shifted his gaze to Beverley. "But first, we'll see you safe to your door."

Irina's cheeks burned at the implication, as well as the memory of their shared kiss in the parking lot, and the thought of him spending another night in her house. He wasn't the only one who'd found last night long.

CHAPTER FOUR

IRINA COULDN'T THINK OF a single thing to say in the car on the ride home, so she concentrated on staying awake. Finishing that second bottle of wine, especially on a Friday night when she was already exhausted from a bad week, had been ill-advised.

Kale seemed OK with the lack of conversation. He'd pushed his seat all the way back to make room for his legs. He kept his eyes on the road and the mirrors, relaxed but alert. The tires hummed on the pavement beneath them. Traffic was light on the highway.

She settled deeper in her seat. While she was far from as mellow as he seemed to be, the wine had done wonders for calming her nerves. The last few days had been hard ones, but at least her fear had receded. Her awareness of Kale had multiplied tenfold however. She tried not to think of the long night ahead, alone with him in her house. She studied his profile in the faint glow from the instrument panel on the dashboard.

"You're staring," he said.

"You're very beautiful." The words slipped out because they were what she'd been thinking. She wished she could retract them. Maybe they'd been too slurred for recognition.

A hint of a smile softened the hard line of his jaw. He

slid her a sidelong look. "That's supposed to be my line."

"I wasn't giving you a line, I was making an observation." She curled her bare toes under the dash. At some point, she wasn't sure when, she'd kicked off her shoes. Her brain, highly reliable in most situations, was having trouble formulating the right words for this one. "You know what I meant."

"Possibly. It's your point I'm not sure of."

Since she wasn't sure of it either, and she'd already made a fool of herself, she might as well carry on. "You're obviously smart as well as attractive. You could have done anything. So why did you choose a career with CSIS? Why become an intelligence officer?"

"Why did you choose to design nuclear weapons systems placement?" he countered.

"I more or less fell into it. I like working with computers and I simply followed the opportunities being offered to me."

"You mean you followed the money."

He said it with enough neutrality that it was obvious he didn't approve. She couldn't fault him for having an opinion. Her work wasn't popular with a lot of people. She supposed with Canada's spy agency, even less. Still, defensiveness tightened her stomach even as she admitted the truth.

"I did. I support my parents," she hastened to add. "My father defected from Russia when he was a young man. He'd been a combination of journalist and translator—we don't have the equivalent in Canada—but after he arrived here he couldn't find work, so he drove a cab in Regina. My mother's Canadian. She developed Guillan-Barré syndrome when I was twenty and he's been her primary caregiver for the past twelve years. They gave up a lot to make sure I had better opportunities than they did. Now it's my turn to look after them. Besides, I like what I do. It's always interesting. Although granted, maybe it's a little too interesting right now." If she hadn't been drinking, she'd never have told him about her parents. She rarely spoke of her private life. Canada's relations with Russia had grown increasingly strained over the past few years and she was uneasy with too many people knowing she had family connections—even though they were stated in her security clearances. Kale, however, could find out anything he wanted about her. He might even already know all of this. CSIS would have investigated her before they gave an intelligence officer this assignment. They'd want to know her background and who might be in it. She tugged at the hem of her skirt, which somehow had hiked up a few inches too far. "Back to you. Why CSIS?"

"Same as you, I guess. They recruited me. It sounded like fun." He navigated into the lane for the next exit off the highway. They were ten minutes from her house.

The wine made her bold. "CSIS recruits only the best. So what's your superpower?"

He shifted gears and veered right at the bottom of the ramp, checking his mirrors and merging with traffic. The slow rise of his lips sketched the hint of a smile. "No superpowers, I'm afraid. I'm good with languages."

That wasn't at all what she'd expected to hear. She'd thought he'd claim to be some kind of mixed martial arts expert—but to be fair, she'd jumped to that conclusion because of his size and the black eye. She'd also assumed he was telling the truth when he told George his background was in kinesiology. Why would someone lie about that? It was such an insignificant detail.

Her curiosity about him, already high, was further piqued. "What languages do you speak?"

"French, Hindi, Farsi, and Urdu, as well as modern Standard Arabic and seven of its dialects."

She blinked. "Prove it to me. Say something in Urdu."

He uttered a string of unintelligible but very lovely

sounding words he couldn't possibly be faking. He cast another sidelong look her way. "In case you're curious, I said, 'Peace be upon you, lovely lady. You are very suspicious by nature.' See? I'm more than just a pretty face."

She'd touched a nerve by calling him beautiful. As a woman, she could well understand how offensive it was. But she sensed he wasn't offended so much as trying to shift the conversation—and she'd love to know why. Other than French, these weren't languages one would expect an average Canadian student to study—and he'd learned them before he joined CSIS, not after.

"I can't really see you blending in with a crowd in Pakistan," she prodded.

"Gathering intelligence isn't always about blending in. Sometimes stereotypes make the best covers. When it comes to my skillset, I don't fit a typical profile."

No, he didn't. And it explained why he said he'd studied kinesiology. Based on appearances alone, it was easy enough to believe.

"Besides, I don't gather intelligence in places like Pakistan." He braked at the entrance to her subdivision, allowing an approaching vehicle to pass by before turning in. Its headlights lit up their car's interior as it went by. "I work mostly in Western urban centers where multinationals tend to congregate."

"So your job is to eavesdrop on people's conversations?"

"More or less. And that," he added, "is more than you need to know, even if your security clearances are better than mine. Shame on you, Dr. Glasov. You're nosy when you drink. Next subject."

She'd been put in her place, but in a manner that left her smiling inside. Personable as well as gorgeous. Kale Martin had great people skills.

They'd reached her driveway. She felt around under

the dash with her toes until she found her shoes, then wriggled them onto her feet. The car rolled to a stop and she opened the door to get out. As she did, she got her arm tangled up in the seat belt assembly.

Before she could extricate herself, Kale had come around the front of the car to help. He held her elbow as she got both feet on the ground. Except for a neighbor's dog barking, no doubt at a squirrel or raccoon, the night was quiet. He got her laptop out of the backseat of the car and slung it over his shoulder.

The knot she'd fashioned her hair into that morning had long since ceased to be neat and tidy. A warm breeze, smelling of damp grass and turned earth, ruffled the stray tendrils sticking to the nape of her neck. He tugged one strand loose with the tip of a finger. She couldn't imagine why she'd been so nervous of him. Right now he was someone to lean on. Literally.

"Thank you," she said, a little too breathlessly. "I'm not usually this clumsy."

"I'm going to go out on a limb and assume you aren't much of a drinker either."

"Is it that obvious?"

One of his arms came around her, helping her stay upright as they walked toward the steps leading to the side kitchen door. His voice shook with the laughter he couldn't quite hold back.

"Well, now. I am a highly trained observer. But even if I were blind, the answer would still have to be yes. Yes, it is."

She was torn between laughter and embarrassment. "Sorry about that."

Immediately, the light teasing tone turned to one of understanding. "Don't be. You've had a rough week. Everyone needs to unwind."

The reminder sobered her up a little. A question had been niggling at the back of her mind, bothering her all evening. "What if whoever accessed my computer already got what they wanted?"

"Then you'd have nothing more to worry about."

That would be nice. But simply because the problem was no longer hers didn't mean it didn't exist, and she felt responsible. Her data should have been better protected.

She frowned. It *was* well protected. "I can't think of anything they might have gotten off my office PC that would be of any use."

They stopped at the foot of the short flight of steps. He let his arm fall to his side. She wobbled a little as she started to dig in her purse for her keys.

"And...we're back to my original theory. Maybe it's personal," he said.

She gave up on finding the keys and handed him her purse. "If it came down to a choice as to which would be more worth the effort, my work or me, as much as it pains me to admit it, my work is the likeliest candidate."

"I disagree. Well," he amended. "When you're being all 'Dr. Glasov' you're a little uptight and self-important. But you know what they say about still waters. I'm confident most men would find your depths well worth exploring."

Moths fluttered against the yard light above the door, casting shadows that stretched into the semi-darkness beyond the carport. She hadn't been able to find her keys because he'd been driving. He already had them in his hand.

"Do I come across as self-important?" she asked.

"I read it as insecurity."

He was so wrong. She wasn't insecure when it came to her work. Social situations that didn't involve other scientists or research projects were a different story entirely. And she had no experience at all with men like Kale. "For a woman, sometimes being smart can be tough."

"For a man, being beautiful ain't no picnic either."

He was making fun of her. She liked it. Scientists might be smart, but they weren't always clever. He stretched her intellect in whole different ways. "Really? I'm sure you had no trouble getting a date for your high school prom."

"Don't tell me your cousin took you to yours."

"I didn't go to my prom. I was fourteen. It was past my bedtime." That was another confession she wouldn't normally have made. At the time she'd been crushed. But being smart didn't equal maturity, and when she looked back on it, she really had been too young. Her parents had made the right decision by keeping her home.

"*Fourteen?*"

The way he said it made her feel like a freak. "Someone didn't do his homework."

Wait.

He hadn't. She squinted at him, sobering a little faster. "Why didn't you know that?"

There was the briefest of hesitations. If she hadn't been looking for it, she might well have missed it.

"Because you aren't under investigation."

"But I'm part of it," she said. "And a significant piece too. Which means one of two things—either you aren't working for CSIS, or CSIS isn't working on the information I gave you. You've been lying to me."

She'd had too much to drink. He'd assumed that meant Dr. Glasov, her official persona, had checked out for the night.

He wouldn't be making that mistake again.

They faced each other, still standing quite close. She had to tip her head so far back to glare at him that he was ready to grab her if she fell over. That light dusting of freckles across the bridge of her nose was really distracting. She was cute when she was indignant. And a whole lot of fun to torment.

Because she wasn't afraid of him anymore.

She had no idea how much that small but significant gesture of trust on her part made him feel. He was tempted to kiss her again, but knew better than to make any move as stupid as that.

"I lie for a living," he hedged. "That's what CSIS does."

"You aren't supposed to be lying to *me*. What's going on?"

He tucked her purse under his arm and placed his hand over his heart. "I swear I'm not lying to you."

"Why should I believe you?" she demanded. "You just said you lie for a living."

A pale gray moth, delicate and light, landed in her hair. He flicked it away with a careful sweep of his fingers. "You can't talk about your work," he reminded her. "I can't talk about mine either. I guess you're going to have to trust your instincts right now."

She held out her hand. "My instincts say to get my house keys and my laptop and tell you to sleep in your car."

He dangled the keys above her head, an inch or so out of her reach. "You're a mean drunk, Dr. Glasov. I was up most of last night. I spent the past five hours driving you around and waiting for you. I was really looking forward to sleeping on that fluffy pink sofa of yours, not in the backseat of my car. Besides, we're supposed to be a couple. What will the neighbors think?"

Her gaze sharpened. "I think we should see other people."

So-o-o tempted to kiss her... Like hell her work was the likeliest candidate for someone to be harassing her.

"Look at us. We're having our first fight. And do you know what the first rule for couple fights is? Never go to bed angry."

He shouldn't push her this way, or tease her and flirt with her. She really believed he'd kissed her in the parking lot as part of their cover. She'd graduated high school at *fourteen.* She might be highly educated academically, but when it came to boy-girl relationships, she'd skipped the core classes. She didn't know what the rules were. She could be too easily hurt by someone like him. He hadn't had a serious girlfriend since college because he was never in the same city for long.

There were reasons he shouldn't get involved with her either. His career was as important to him as hers was to her. He believed in the work he was doing. He wanted world peace.

So yeah, maybe he thought his job was a teensy bit more important than hers.

"Tell you what," he relented. "This isn't a conversation we should be having right now. You let me sleep on your sofa, and in the morning after we're both better rested, we'll have a serious talk while you're making me breakfast."

That would give him a few uninterrupted hours to do some discreet investigating into her background, and by investigating, he meant snooping through her personal belongings. Her mention of a Russian father hadn't escaped his notice. He wondered how much she knew about his history. If he was Cold War era, then as a journalist, he'd most likely worked for his government. He would also have been young, and quite possibly idealistic, although Kale didn't know enough about him or his circumstances for an accurate profile. Chances were good that he'd been some sort of spy, but given Irina's security clearances, he'd also been debriefed and cleared by the Canadian government.

Which meant nothing. People passed those clearances every day. Irina's career, too, would have progressed faster than her background checks could be updated. And tensions between Canada and Russia had increased in recent years. She might not find her next security clearance as easy to pass.

Her current situation wasn't going to help.

"Now I'm making you breakfast?" she asked, drawing his thoughts back to the matter at hand. "If you're supposed to be my boyfriend, why shouldn't you be making breakfast for me?"

She was arguing for the sake of it and he couldn't let that one pass. She made it too easy. "You'd have to earn one of mine, Dr. Babe."

"Maybe you'd have to earn one of mine too."

He raised an eyebrow, bringing pink to her cheeks. The light above the door caught the clear, guileless green of her eyes. She sucked at this game, and although the wine could take part of the blame, it was mostly because she was the furthest thing from a casual hookup he could imagine. Dr. Glasov was all business. Irina was…sweet.

The kind of girl a guy married.

And that was the problem. He really wanted to kiss her but couldn't come up with an excuse to do so. If he did anyway, he'd be raising expectations. She deserved better from him. He wasn't a player.

He tossed the keys in the flat of his palm. "Why don't we flip a coin in the morning to see which one of us has to make breakfast?"

"That's probably best."

It sounded like disappointment he heard, buried beneath her speedy agreement, but that might be ego on his part.

He fitted the key in the lock and hustled her into the kitchen. Even before he had time to find the light switch, she'd kicked off her shoes in the soft, murky gloom.

"If I ever take up a second career, it's going to be designing women's shoes," she sighed, peering down at her bare, slender feet and wiggling her toes. "How come we can put people into space but no one has come up with comfortable heels that are both fashionable and affordable?"

"You could try wearing shoes that don't have three-inch heels instead."

He liked them though. They drew the eye up the length of her legs, which were no hardship to stare at, to the prim hemline of her narrow skirt. From there, his imagination took over. The red skirt cupped a very fine ass. The white T-shirt cradled more curves. The jacket that matched her skirt was in the backseat of her car, he recalled. He'd have to remember to get that for her tomorrow.

"Spoken like a man who isn't vertically challenged." She pulled the elastic from her hair. With a ruffle of her fingers and a shake of her head, a thick mass of caramel tresses cascaded around her shoulders.

Like that wasn't hot. His brain drifted south.

He located the switch on the wall and the light fixture over the kitchen table blinked on.

Irina walked to the fridge. Would you like something to eat?" She glanced at him in dismay, her hand on the latch. "I never thought. Did you get any dinner? Or did you wait in the car the whole evening?"

"I ate." He'd had a bag of potato chips and a bottle of soda. "But I won't say no if you're offering to make me another one of those smoked meat sandwiches. You aren't off the hook over breakfast though. We're still flipping that coin."

"Duly noted."

She got the ingredients from the fridge and the cupboard and piled them on the island while he sat at the table and watched her work. She had a way of focusing all her attention on a task, and attacking it with precision, that he enjoyed. He could well imagine what it would be like to have all that concentration leveled on him. He'd bet she was worth making breakfast for. Probably more than once, too.

She stifled a yawn with the heel of her hand. He checked his watch under the table. Barely ten o'clock on a Friday night. Irina Glasov was no party girl. Not by a long stretch of the imagination. Meanwhile, he was wide awake.

She reached to take a plate off a shelf, stretching on her bare toes, exposing a midriff that had him licking his lips as the hem of her T-shirt parted ways with the waistband of her skirt. She loaded the plate with two neatly-cut triangles and set the thick sandwich before him.

"I must seem so boring to you," she said.

"Why would you think that?" That wasn't at all the impression she gave him.

She shrugged, a seemingly casual motion on the surface that in reality was anything but. "I sit at a computer all day. I'm ready for bed by ten o'clock."

Now he felt like a jerk. She'd seen him checking his watch. "Being ready for bed doesn't make a woman boring. In fact, it makes her a whole lot more interesting to a man."

Her eyes lost some of the haziness brought on by stress, fatigue, and too much wine with her dinner. "You like to bait me too. I'm glad I can provide entertainment on what's got to be a very dull assignment for you."

If there was one thing he'd figured out about her already it was that Irina had her fair share of pride. The trouble was that it was threaded through with thin veins of feminine insecurity, and without meaning to, he'd managed to offend her. She thought her intelligence was her most appealing feature. It certainly wasn't the least of them. But even brainy women liked to know men found them attractive. Joking with her right now was the wrong path for him to be taking.

"You aren't boring, Irina. Far from it. I enjoy teasing you because you're so fascinating."

Her brow furrowed as she processed his words.

She ran her fingertips along the edge of the tabletop before turning abruptly away. "You don't have to sleep on the sofa. You can use the spare room at the end of the hall. The bed's already made. I'll see you in the morning. Good night."

She didn't believe him. Suddenly, it became very important to him that she did.

"Hang on a second."

The chair legs sputtered against the floor as he pushed away from the table. His head hit the light fixture, sending it swinging. He steadied it with one hand. She'd left the kitchen and entered the hall that led to the back of the house by the time he caught up with her.

"Irina. Wait."

She stopped in front of her open bedroom door, her reluctance to continue the conversation etched on her pretty features. He could tell the second Dr. Glasov took charge. Her eyebrows rose and those intriguing green eyes widened in the dim light to form an unspoken question that exuded irritation. *What is it now?*

He had to bite the inside of his cheek to keep from saying exactly what it was that he had on his mind. With her feet and legs bare, her hair tumbled around her shoulders, and her skirt slightly askew, she couldn't look any sexier if she tried.

Or less like a world famous computer scientist who designed nuclear weapons systems placements in aircraft. The contradictions suckered him in. How many women like this could there possibly be in the world?

So much for that plausible excuse he was lacking. He was going to kiss her without one.

They were alone in her house though, right outside her bedroom, and she didn't know him very well. He was a lot bigger than she was and he hadn't forgotten how nervous of him she'd been, or that alcohol played a significant part in her bravery tonight. It might be best if he kept his hands to himself.

But she made it so hard.

"You have a bit of mustard on your chin," he lied. She lifted her fingers to her face, trying to feel where it might be. "Not there. Here."

He bent his head and pressed his lips to the corner of her mouth, offering a soft, gentle caress. A breath of a sigh—a tiny exhalation of air—brushed his cheek in response. She shifted ever so slightly, whether by accident or design he couldn't be sure, but either way, her mouth glided beneath his until full contact was made. She tugged on his lower lip, the tip of her tongue stroking against it.

Fireworks exploded inside his brain. He'd meant to come across as nonthreatening. To let her set the pace. Dr. Glasov, however, could kiss.

She was as attracted to him as he was to her. Of that much he was certain. While the timing wasn't the best, and he'd never coax her into doing anything she might regret in the morning, he wasn't about to pass up an opportunity he might regret missing either. But they each needed to be clear on what they were willing to offer. There had to be boundaries.

He planted his palms on the wall behind her, backing her up against it, not in order to pin her in place, but to keep his hands off her. He teased her lips farther open, dipping his tongue between them. Her fingers found his hips, her thumbs cuddling too close to his pelvis for comfort. In an instant, an erection strained at the fly of his jeans, begging for freedom. All his good intentions drifted away on the wave of heat flooding his groin.

He broke off the kiss. Wow. Things were moving a lot faster than he'd expected. His lungs bellowed like he'd just run ten kilometers. He couldn't quite catch his breath. His ability to form complete sentences also seemed somewhat impaired.

He flicked one thumb across the corner of her mouth, swiping at the imaginary mustard stain. "Think I got it."

"Thank you. I can't imagine how it got there."

His mouth crooked into a grin at her prim, thinly-veiled sarcasm. She was an open book. Not a simple one, granted. More a thick Russian literature translation complete with footnotes and an annotated bibliography. He liked that about her. He liked it a lot. "You're the brains in the room. Try making an educated guess."

She tilted her head to one side, casting him a quizzical look. "My guess is that there never was any mustard."

"Really? Why would I lie about something like that?"

"You tell me. You're the one who lies for a living."

She ducked under his arm and into the bedroom, shutting the door in his face before he had a chance to respond.

He had not seen that coming.

He stared at the closed door for a long, incredulous moment, listening to her light steps as she moved around the room. Another door closed. A tap opened wide in the ensuite bathroom inside. He had no difficulty imagining her bedtime routine—the glide of a damp cloth over her skin, a brush stroking those long, silky tresses of hair.

He rapped his forehead against the door frame a few times, summoning his brain back from its southern migration.

She didn't suck at this game quite as much as he'd thought.

CHAPTER FIVE

IRINA AWOKE WITH A mouth that tasted like garbage and a brain attempting to drill its way free through her eyeballs.

It took a few seconds of staring at the bedroom ceiling fan above the bed for her to figure out the cause of the overwhelming mortification she felt. He was clanging pots in the kitchen, singing a truly horrible rendition of a popular song favored by pre-teenage girls. She'd find his taste in music funny if she wasn't so hung over.

Or feeling so foolish. She'd told him he was beautiful. She'd let him kiss her. She'd kissed him back. Then she'd shut the bedroom door in his face.

Her friend Beverley gave terrible advice. If last night had proven anything, it was that Kale Martin was the last man she should go for. He was far too much...everything.

He was also lying to her.

She examined the facts. Her professional biography—out there for the entire world to see—clearly stated she'd graduated from high school at the age of fourteen. If he'd done any research on her at all, that was a fact he couldn't possibly have missed. To her, that suggested his investigation wasn't official.

But Detective Buchanan had confirmed Kale was with

CSIS. And he hadn't faked speaking Urdu. She'd been to Pakistan and he had the inflections down pat. He *knew* people too. He understood what motivated them. From the moment he first stepped into her kitchen he'd done his best to put her at ease.

And then to knock her off balance.

The thought of the kiss—kisses—they'd shared left her awash in a full-body blush that prickled to the roots of her hair. Those certainly had nothing to do with any official investigation. Not that she had a right to complain. She'd been an active and enthusiastic participant last night, and if he hadn't stopped, she wouldn't have either. That was another mark in his favor, although she gave it up grudgingly. She might not have initiated the kiss, but she wished she'd been the one to show some restraint.

OK. She believed he was legitimate when it came to his work. So what was his game? If CSIS wasn't actively investigating her complaint, then why was he here?

That was the problem with spies. One could never be sure what they were really after. He was never going to tell her the truth so there was no point in demanding an explanation from him. Bottom line, she felt better about having him here. Safer.

But only up to a point.

She rolled to her side, tangling her legs in the cotton sheet she'd thrown off in the night. A tall glass of water sat on the bedside table, along with a roll of antacids. The gesture was thoughtful. The fact that he'd been in her room while she was asleep?

Disconcerting. She'd skipped pajamas and slept in a tank top and panties. He must have gotten an eyeful.

A glance at the clock said it was quarter to nine. She sat up and chewed four of the antacids before chugging the whole glass of water. Under-hydrating had been her biggest mistake of the night, but at least her stomach had settled. It rumbled at the smell of bacon wafting through the cracks around her door.

Footsteps in the hall, then a light knock on the door, made her sit up straighter in bed. The quiet sound of her name had her clutching the sheet to her chest.

"Irina? You awake?"

"Almost," she called back.

A low rumble of laughter stirred up the butterflies already fluttering hard in her chest. "Breakfast is ready in ten minutes."

Enough time to get decent. Not enough for a shower.

She sprawled on her back on the bed, one hand splayed on her stomach, the other arm flung over her head. She had an upcoming conference in Paris to prepare for. She was sitting on a panel with eight other scientists and needed to check her phone messages and email. They came from all over the world and most didn't keep the same schedules. A lot of them couldn't tell what time of day it was in their own area codes, let alone the day of the week, when they were involved in a project. She, too, was guilty as charged.

Her phone and laptop, however, were both in the bag Kale had left beside a chair at the kitchen table. She wondered if he'd tried to go through them. Everything was password-protected, but if he asked for access, she'd give it to him. She didn't keep sensitive data on her personal hard drives.

She made a trip to the bathroom to rinse out her mouth and grab some acetaminophen for her headache before digging through a dresser drawer in search of a clean pair of shorts and a T-shirt. It only took a minute to clip her hair up with a plastic claw. She'd wash it later. After she made her bed and hung up her discarded clothes from the previous night, her ten minutes were up. The thought of Kale in her kitchen, however, remained overwhelming.

She'd have to face him eventually and might as well get it over with.

He stood at the stove with a spatula in his hand, his white shirt unbuttoned and the tails hanging free, the sleeves rolled up his forearms past his elbows to biceps as thick as her thighs. His feet were bare. He'd tidied his hair, the blond man bun smoothed into place.

He was gorgeous. She could watch him all day.

A hunger shot through her that had nothing to do with food. The attraction between them wasn't a figment of her imagination. Since she appeared to be enough woman for him, why should he be too much man for her?

As Beverley had said, why not have fun?

He glanced up from stirring the contents of the frying pan. Morning light caught the incredible blue of his eyes. The gleam in them suggested he knew what she'd been thinking and that his thoughts were running along the same lines.

"Hey, there. How'd you sleep?"

"Like the dead."

His lips quirked into a sly, sexy grin. "You were breathing. I checked."

There wasn't much she could say about that. She wanted to have fun, yes, but she'd never be able to pull it off to the same level he did. She couldn't change who she was—a dull and boring computer scientist.

Her gaze flitted from his to settle on her laptop bag. She wandered over and dug in one of the side pockets for her phone, then sat down to go through her messages.

"Your breakfast is getting cold."

She looked up from her phone, startled to discover that while she'd been reading, the table had been set with placemats and napkins and he'd served her bacon and scrambled eggs. A glass of orange juice sweated beside her plate. Coffee steamed in a mug. He sat across from her, blue eyes studying her face, his own plate half empty.

"Sorry," she said. "I sometimes get lost when I'm working."

"No kidding. I tap danced and sang show tunes before I finally gave up trying to get your attention." He pointed his fork at her breakfast. "Now put the phone away and eat. We have rules in this house."

"Yes, sir." She set the phone beside her plate. He raised his eyebrows and flattened his lips with such an expression of mock patience that she had to smile. She picked up the phone and tucked it into the laptop bag pocket. "Let me guess. Your mother was strict about mealtimes."

"When we managed to sit down at the same time as a family, yes. You better believe it. Those were rare events and she kept them special. She raised four sons. We're all terrified of her."

"The giantess Jord must be fearsome, indeed."

He paused in the act of spearing a piece of bacon. "You think my mother's a Norse goddess?"

"No one's ever compared you to Thor before?" She found that hard to believe.

"Well…yeah," he admitted. "But they think Thor's mother's name is Frigga, after the comic book character. You know. The one in the Avengers movies?"

"I've never seen those movies," Irina confessed. She'd heard of them though. She spent her work days with nerds after all.

"What kind of movies do you like to watch, then?"

"I don't really have a preference. I usually read." Making her the biggest nerd ever.

"I've seen your reading material." He made a gesture as if he were hanging himself. "You need to expand your horizons. We're going to watch a movie tonight."

That sounded...cozy. "Aren't we supposed to be working? Trying to find out what's going on with those pop-ups on my computer?" She reached for her coffee. "And what about that talk you said we'd have?" She threw that out there to see how he'd react.

He set his fork down and pushed his plate out of the way so he could rest his forearms on the table. "That's right. I promised you an explanation, didn't I?" He leaned toward her as if preparing to impart important state secrets. "OK. Here's the deal. I've been working nonstop for the past six or seven weeks. Right now I'm not at the top of my game. I might have missed a few things. I'm willing to bet you'd work twenty-four seven if you didn't need to sleep, too. We could both use a break. This province has a beach that's world famous for surfing and I'm not planning to miss out on it. So guess where we're headed today? Bring a book if you like. Tonight, we're ordering pizza and watching movies. Unless, of course, you can think of a better way for us to unwind?"

Not at the top of his game, hmm? She begged to differ. Was he trying to tell her that he'd missed important information? That he wasn't as prepared to handle an investigation as he might otherwise have been? Or was he simply trying to misdirect her?

Common sense leaned toward misdirection. Under the table, she flexed her hands. Then, she drew a few breaths. She didn't have a clue how to figure him out. He wasn't at all the person he presented to the world. So the next question became, did she trust him?

Yes and no. She believed he was CSIS. As for the rest

of his game, the jury was out. For example, she was only ninety-five percent sure how he'd meant for her to take that last remark, and even then, only because she factored in the kisses they'd shared. The odds still weren't quite high enough for her, however, so she hedged her response. "I'm good with whatever you'd like to do."

The heat in his eyes tipped the odds to one hundred percent. "You say that, Dr. Babe. But wait until tonight rolls around."

Forget the other games he might have going on. This one was about sex, plain and simple. Now she had to decide if she was willing to play along.

Why not have fun?

She couldn't change who she was. But she could choose to be brave. While subtlety wasn't her strength, and she wasn't quick-witted with comebacks, she knew how to stand her ground and be direct. She met his gaze and held it, the same as she would if she'd been challenged by a peer during a presentation. "I'd only change my mind if you gave me a good reason to."

The incredulity slackening his jaw signaled she'd caught him off guard. Worry that she'd misread him dampened her palms. Perhaps he hadn't been serious. Maybe she was a challenge who'd turned out to be no challenge at all.

He found his voice. "In that case, I'll be on my best behavior all day. Guaranteed."

A heady sense of relief, and perhaps triumph that, while she might feel awkward and uncertain around him, she could hold her own nonetheless, replaced her worry. Then, some of her bravery began to erode. Directness was one thing. Daring was a whole different ball game.

"I can see you thinking, Irina." His expression gentled, at odds with the awe-inspiring, muscled bulk of him. He'd straightened one of his long legs so that a bare foot, high-arched and well-shaped, rested disconcertingly close to her chair. Whether he did it intentionally or not, he constantly invaded her personal space. "Stop analyzing everything I say. There's no need for it. When I watch movies with a woman, she gets control of the remote. It has a stop button."

She could feel her face flaming. She really hoped they were talking about the same thing. "I'm not very good at picking out movies. I don't watch very many."

"Yeah. I figured that out. Don't worry so much. You have plenty of time to make a selection. Remotes have pause buttons too. Now finish your breakfast," he said, picking up his fork once again. "This morning we're going surfing."

They stopped at the surf shop closest to the beach so Kale could arrange for a rental board. A short time after that, he was struggling into his wetsuit and getting ready to hit the waves.

A brisk wind blew off the ocean. Irina, beside him, carried a canvas bag containing a magazine, a beach towel, water bottles and sandwiches. He'd insisted she leave her laptop at home. She set the bag on the sand near the rocks at the high water point. Those rocks created a natural barrier between the beach and the road, so that the busy parking lot was hidden from sight, creating a sense of isolation.

He couldn't keep his eyes off her. Dressed in a cream-colored, cable-knit sweater that draped off one shoulder, and navy Bermuda shorts, she was slender in a petite, sleekly feminine way that had heat searing through him at unexpected moments, like now.

He pried his thoughts away from all the movie euphemisms they'd made over breakfast. She'd been playing with him, fighting fire with fire. She was far too skittish around him and had too much pride to be serious. While academically he was no slouch, he was hardly on the same level she was.

That didn't mean he wasn't going to see how far she'd go. He'd meant it when he'd said they both needed a break and she was quite the diversion. He itched to run his fingers over all that silky, lightly-tanned skin.

Gulls circled and squawked in the wide blue sky overhead. A frown crinkled her pixie nose and turned the full, pink curve of her lips upside down.

"The signs say it's not safe to swim here," she said, shielding her eyes with her hand as she stared out at the stretch of sparkling gray ocean.

Swimming was off-limits here because there weren't any lifeguards. He'd done enough surfing in the area to know better than to ignore the posted signs that warned of dangerous currents, but there were three other surfers who looked like they knew what they were doing in the water already. They'd keep an eye on each other.

He zipped up the front of the wetsuit. "The tide's on its way in. I'm good for a few hours. But just in case, the car keys are in my jeans pocket."

Green eyes swiveled to his. "That's not funny. I'm serious."

"So am I." It touched him that she was concerned. No one but his mother ever worried about him, and even she had given up a long time ago. He made a few phone calls a year, mostly to make up for the Christmases and birthdays he sometimes missed, and she was happy. "See those rocks?" He wrapped an arm around Irina's shoulders and turned her so she faced the farthest one of the two points that formed the small cove where they stood. "No one surfs beyond there. As long as the tide's coming in and I stay on this side of the rocks, I'll be fine."

Doubt curled the corners of her lips downward. "If you say so."

She didn't believe him. That was pretty cute too.

An unsettling rush of possessiveness took him by surprise when she tipped her face upward as if about to say something more. She was small, the top of her ponytail barely reaching his chest. He dropped a light kiss on her mouth, sweeping his tongue across those full, frowning lips to steal a taste of the salt on her skin from the fresh ocean air. When he lifted his head, her green eyes were wide and bemused.

He knew the feeling.

"Do you think we might be carrying this whole pretend relationship a little too far?" she asked.

The short answer was yes.

He still had an arm around her. He shrugged before letting go of her to pick up his board, struggling for cool. "What can I say? I'm a touchy kind of guy." He straightened. "Is that going to be a problem for you?"

Unsmiling, she gave the cheeky challenge far more consideration than it deserved. "No."

Her answer was as honest and direct as he'd come to expect of her. It was his reaction to it that he hadn't anticipated. His brain dried up and his reeling thought processes shifted straight to his crotch.

He'd been so wrong to think she was no good at this game. The problem for him was that she didn't play by regulation rules and he had no idea what his next move should be.

Other than the three surfers out on the water, they were alone. "Stay here where I can see you," he said, suddenly bothered by the thought of her sitting by herself on the beach. She was safe enough. The beach wasn't really deserted. There was plenty of traffic right over the ridge.

Still.

She held up a copy of *American Scientist* magazine. "I've got my entertainment right here."

His uneasiness passed. No one who knew anything about her would ever, not for one single moment, suspect she'd be spending the day at a beach famous for surfing.

"If that's your idea of entertainment," he said, "then you don't get to pick out the movie tonight."

He carried the board to the water's edge where he straightened the cords on the kite before wading in. It took him an embarrassing number of tries to get it into the air. He needed to concentrate on what he was doing and not let his attention keep wandering to the confusing woman watching him from the beach.

Once he had the kite up and was out on the water the rest of the world slipped away. A storm had been blowing out in the Atlantic Ocean last night, and today, the waves crashing against the shoreline were unusually high. He loved the sensation of flying as his board shot off the crests.

He had to change directions to get out of the path of another surfer who was headed straight for him and he made a hard landing. His foot slipped off the board, sending him sliding into the water. A wave washed over his head, pushing him down. He bobbed to the surface a few yards from his board, sputtering water and shaking his hair out of his eyes. The kite dipped and danced in the sky. It hadn't yet fallen but was on its way down. He shot a glance toward Irina's distant form on the beach, wondering if she'd seen him go under and if she was worried.

She was no longer alone. A man in a bright neon orange-and-blue wetsuit was walking from the path that led to the parking lot and down the beach toward her. A surfboard had been jammed upright in the sand at the foot of the path. She didn't lift her head from her magazine. So far, she was oblivious.

Kale was too far from the beach, and the water too rough, for him to get a good idea of what was going on, but whatever it was, he didn't like it. While a great deal of his objection was territorial—she was a beautiful woman, after all, and he was a typical man—being approached by a stranger would unsettle her. She counted on him for protection. And he wasn't where he should be.

He scrambled back on his board and set out for shore, zigzagging into the wind. Another one of the surfers who'd been in the water was also on the beach now, but he was packing up his kite and had his back to Irina and the newcomer. Kale jumped off his board and waded out of the water, tugging on the cords and bringing his kite in too. He dropped everything in the wet sand and walked toward Irina and her companion.

The stranger was speaking to her. She tipped her head to the side, her expression warily polite. Then she smiled at him, looking pretty and sweet. She held up the magazine for the stranger's inspection. Jealousy swirled in Kale's stomach. That was the same pick-up he'd chosen to explain how he and Irina had met.

This guy was so unoriginal.

But something about him seemed familiar. As Kale got closer, he understood why. It was Extreme Sports Guy, the investment banker he'd been tailing for weeks. What were the chances?

Pretty good, all things considered.

And he should have considered them. Starting a new assignment back to back in the same area as the last one hadn't been a smart move on his part. Bringing Irina to the beach with him was even less so. There were only so many beaches for surfing this close to the city and Lawrencetown was the best.

Extreme Sports Guy looked his way when he realized someone was approaching. Kale saw the exact instant of recognition. The banker shot a glance between him and Irina. A slow, knowing grin spread across his face.

"Well, well. Isn't this a surprise?" he said to Kale. "No deliveries today?"

Fury prickled the backs of Kale's eyes. The bastard would have been warned about him, and the shit-eating, arrogant grin said he'd been told not to worry.

They'd see about that. He reached for his jeans, neatly folded on one of the black rocks, and dug the keys from his pocket. He tossed them to Irina. "Go wait in the car. Lock the doors. I'll be along as soon as I pack up my board."

One of the things he appreciated about her was that she was smart enough to know when not to argue. With a worried, fleeting look at him over her shoulder, she silently gathered her things and did as she was told. He watched her walk across the sand, the canvas bag in her hand, hips gently swaying, the wind snagging her sweater and hair. Once she was out of earshot, he turned back to the banker, who was watching her too.

"Isn't she just the prettiest little thing?" the banker remarked.

Kale's fury eased, shifting to a cold, icy control. He had at least five inches on the other man and a good thirty pounds. Wrestling had been his varsity sport. He'd had defensive training for work. As a kid, he'd loved to fight.

He let that same gleam shine from his eyes as he replied. "You like to play dangerous sports. Hang out with dangerous people. Let's see how tough you really are. If anything happens to her—so much as a ding in the fender of her car—you'll be the first person I come after. And you're stupid easy to find. You think about that before you go mentioning anything about her to any of your friends."

"Hey." The banker put his hands in the air, backing up a few steps. "There's nothing to talk about. I saw a pretty woman sitting alone and figured she was here to hook up with surfers. You can't blame me for trying. How was I supposed to know someone was already nailing her?" He couldn't seem to resist getting in another dig. "Who'd have guessed a smart, pretty woman like that would do a delivery boy?"

If Extreme Sports Guy had any inkling he was messing with CSIS he'd be far less cocky than this. He and his friends all likely assumed Kale was undercover RCMP. The guy had such an ugly surprise in store for him. If he went near Irina again, he'd have an uglier one still. Kale meant every word he'd said. He had connections too. CSIS protected its own. Unofficially, of course.

But this was the first time Kale had ever needed those kinds of connections and he resented the taste it left in his mouth. He knew how to keep his cool better than this.

"Enjoy your surfing," he said. "The conditions are great."

It took him more time than he liked to gather up his gear and get it all to the parking lot, where Irina had done as he'd told her to and was waiting for him with the car doors locked.

"What was that all about?" she asked when he slid into the driver's seat beside her.

She turned so she faced him, bringing her knee close to his thigh. The inside of the car was warm, but thanks to the cool ocean air, not overly so. She'd cracked the windows a notch and tossed her sweater into the backseat. She wore a white tank top over the navy shorts.

Pretty and practical. Not much wonder she'd caught the banker's interest.

She certainly had his.

As he looked through the rear window so he could back out of the parking space, he edged his leg toward hers so that they were touching. "It had nothing to do with you. A loose end from another project. An unfortunate coincidence. I suggested he try online dating though, because picking up women on beaches might prove hazardous to his health."

She had such an expressive face. It was plain she had no idea how to take his comment—if she should be flattered or afraid, or if it really did have nothing to do with her.

"Don't tell me he was responsible for your black eye," she said.

Her ability to put things together never ceased to amaze him. He'd almost forgotten about it. The bruising had already faded to a faint yellow. "That little sissy? Please. Give me some credit."

She didn't laugh, or even crack a smile for that matter. "He seemed perfectly normal."

"I'm sure he is." They were on the highway by now, driving the short distance to the surf shop so Kale could return the rented equipment. He let out a sigh. "They always are. There's just no way of telling what drives ordinary people to do things, Irina. There are usually a number of reasons, although in my line of work, ninety-nine percent of the time the biggest motivation is money."

"And the other one percent?"

"Ego and ideology. Usually a combination of both." Those were next to impossible to fight. All anyone could do was try to contain them and keep them from spreading.

She arched a brow. "Are those percentages quantified statistics backed up by analysis?"

"More like the qualified results of field observations conducted by an expert," he said. "And equally valid for statistical purposes."

He pulled into the surf shop's tiny parking lot. Gravel crunched under the tires. He didn't want to talk about this anymore. Not with Irina. He didn't like his world touching hers. She was still frowning, concern in her eyes, and he didn't like that either.

"Why Arabic and Urdu?" she asked.

The question, coming so out of the blue, was unexpected. The answer, however, was simple enough. "My dad's a diplomat. We traveled a lot while I was growing up, mostly in the Middle East. In university, here in Canada, I had a lot of Arabic friends. I got their culture and they wanted to learn about mine. It was a simple progression."

He shut off the engine and got out of the car, then leaned back inside. "Today's our day off, Dr. Babe. No more talk about work. Put some thought into what kind of movie you'd like to watch tonight. For what it's worth, my preference is musicals. If it's a zombie musical, you get extra points."

Amusement edged out the concern. "I don't think we could possibly be more different."

And that, Kale thought as he unstrapped the rented gear from the roof of the car, was what he'd best keep in mind.

CHAPTER SIX

HE WAS THE SON of a diplomat. Yet another piece in the fascinatingly complex Kale Martin puzzle.

When he'd spoken to the stranger on the beach he'd morphed into a completely different person from the affable one she was slowly beginning to know. The harsh expression on his face—the ice in his eyes—had shaken her. She'd had no trouble envisioning that Kale Martin tracking terrorists in the back alleys of overcrowded third world cities.

But the realization that she'd seen nothing wrong with the man who'd approached her on a public beach and inquired about her reading material shook her far more. He'd actually quoted a recent article, establishing a rapport with her, and she'd fallen for it. In light of recent events, she would have thought she'd be more street smart than that. Now she got why women went missing every day and how innocent children could be lured away by strangers.

She could also see why Kale was so suspicious of her coworkers. She'd lose her faith in humanity too, if she lived in his world.

She wanted no part of it.

Which meant she was having second thoughts about the expectations she'd raised that morning.

Common sense said to slow down. They'd only met a few days ago.

Unfortunately, the pesky pheromones in the close confines of the car on the drive home were affecting her ability to reason. They shouted that a few days were plenty when all anyone wanted was sex. He wasn't going to be around forever and she had nothing to lose.

She needed some distance. Some room to think.

It was time for supper when they arrived back at her house.

While Kale ordered a pizza, she got out her laptop. He might be able to take an entire day off, but she had that panel in Paris to prepare for and other people's schedules and time zones to factor in. Putting off having to deal with the impending evening was an added incentive for work.

She set the laptop on the table and turned it on. She frowned. It was running slower than normal. She opened her email program, scanned the contents, and found a security alert from the tech department at her office. That was unusual too. They had no reason to send an alert to her private account.

"What's up with the scowl?" Kale flicked off his phone and moved around behind her, peering over her shoulder and scattering her thoughts.

"This."

She indicated the email, trying her best to ignore the hand he placed on the back of her chair and the cheek that was too close to hers as he bent forward to read it. She right-clicked on the header, wanting to check the sender's Internet Protocol address, and discovered it was set to private. That meant the email hadn't come from her office.

"I'm being spammed. Give me a few minutes," she

added, her fingers already flying across the keyboard. "I want to find out where this is really from." It took her longer than she'd expected to track it. When she did, she found not one IP address, but a string of them, all linked together. "Damn."

"I take it something's wrong?"

She'd forgotten all about Kale. He was still standing behind her, looking over her shoulder.

"I've picked up a botnet," she said.

"What's a botnet?"

"It's a web robot—a computer, or in this case a number of computers, that have been taken over by hackers." She kept her explanation simple. "Messages are sent out and received through the network the botnet creates. It's likely gathering personal information from my laptop and relaying it back to the hackers through a string of IP addresses." She sighed, annoyed. "Everyone in my email list is probably infected now too."

"Don't you have firewall protection?"

"Of course I do. I've even installed one I wrote myself. But any program can be compromised if you know what you're doing. Hackers are tech savvy and government websites are favorite targets for them. My guess is that I picked up this botnet when I was doing some online research."

"Any chance it might be related to the pop-ups you were getting at work?"

"There's a very good chance. There's an equal possibility that it's something different entirely."

She really hoped it was different, and this was a random hack, not something targeted specifically at her. She'd begun to believe Kale was right—that she was overreacting to those pop-ups she'd received and that someone at work had been playing a mean prank on her.

More importantly, that was what she wanted to believe.

He'd gone tense, the same way he had at the beach earlier. "Can you find out where it came from?"

"Yes, but it might take some time."

"So much for the movie. I guess we're working tonight after all."

He ran the tip of one finger down the back of her neck, sending shivers the length of her spine and shattering her concentration. Maybe he wasn't as focused on business as she'd assumed. She couldn't figure him out—which, she freely admitted, was a big part of the attraction. But he was an additional stress in her life that she didn't need.

For a few days or weeks, though... That would be an adventure. The shiver turned into a dull, aching throb. Because no. He wouldn't be here forever.

A few minutes later, immersed in her task, she forgot all about him. When she finally resurfaced, the light above the table was on and a cold piece of pizza sat on a plate at her elbow. She had a vague recollection of a delivery.

Kale was leaning against the kitchen island, all long legs and broad shoulders. She had no idea how long he'd been standing there, watching her. The man had patience. He'd also showered. His thick blond hair was loose and still damp. He wore a clean white T-shirt, a bit too tight across the chest, and a pair of black board shorts that showed off long, muscled legs covered in a light dusting of gold. It had to be wrong for him to be this beautiful and intelligent, too. If he had any real flaws, she'd yet to discover them.

"So what did you learn?"

She blinked a few times, rubbing her eyes. "I tracked the intrusion as far as the Russian Business Network."

The RBN was an Internet service provider with links to the Russian Mafia and organized crime. The online businesses operating through it came from all over the world. Most were anonymous, identifiable only by nicknames. CSIS would know of it.

The intrusion on her laptop might be nothing more than an annoyance. Or, it could be very bad news.

"That's as far as I'm going," she added. "There's simply no way of telling where anything leads beyond that. I do know it won't be anywhere good. Whoever did this was professional."

"The RBN. Holy shit." His blue eyes, fixed on her face, grew speculative. "You can't go any farther? Or you won't?"

She was tired, she was worried, and she was testy. He'd objected to her speaking with a man on a public beach, but this was OK?

"I am not hacking into the RBN. There's nothing I keep on my laptop that's worth it. If you want to try, feel free to pass on the information to your tech guys at CSIS. That's what they get paid for."

Her outburst hung in the air between them, its vehemence surprising them both.

His gaze softened to one of sympathy. "Eat your pizza. I need to think about this for a bit."

And she didn't want to think about it any longer. Her head ached. Her back was stiff too. She rolled her neck, trying to loosen the muscles. She'd disappointed him, but hacking into the RBN would be stupid, especially for someone in her line of work. While CSIS involvement might protect her security clearances, she had no desire to draw even more online attention to herself. The possibility of the botnet intrusion being connected to the pop-ups she'd received was also unsettling. Those had been personalized and she couldn't figure out why. What would anyone hope to gain?

"Here." Kale crossed the kitchen. Seconds later his hands were on her shoulders, his thumbs pressing into the trapezius muscles and gently massaging the kinks into puddles of goo. "Let me know if I'm being too rough."

How did he manage to make that sound both considerate and dirty at the same time?

She caught the inside of her cheek with her teeth, her irritation and fears melting away with the heat of his touch, only to be replaced by a very different type of concern. She did her best to ignore it.

"I did find out what website the botnet came from," she offered. "I was looking up international trade restrictions on nuclear exports and one of the links I clicked on must have been infected. You might want to pass that on too."

"We need to talk about broadening your intellectual horizons beyond work," Kale replied. "You seem to be stuck in a rut."

He was so right about that. She considered all the reasons sleeping with him would be a bad idea. Then she thought about all the times she'd passed up on adventure because she was too busy with her education or work. The latter list was depressingly long. What were the odds of another man like this one—exciting, intelligent, and so very gorgeous—touching her life, even briefly?

Her heart, already pounding with nervous anticipation, picked up its pace. She angled her head so that she was looking at him upside down.

"Guess what else I found online?"

"I can't believe you found a zombie musical," Kale said.

She made a face at the flickering screen. "I can't believe it's this bad."

"Really? 'Zombie musical' screamed high art to you?"

It was well past midnight. They'd finished the last of the pizza while they watched the movie. Kale slouched on the sofa beside her, his bare feet propped on her coffee table, hands linked behind his head, almost six and a half feet of testosterone-infused god. His eyes were on her now, not the television, his gaze sliding over her skin in a manner that made her burn in response. Ignoring him was impossible.

That was the only touching he'd done in two hours however. Even though she'd given him the remote, which sat on the cushion between them, he hadn't so much as tried to hold her hand. Her hormones were going haywire from frustration. She'd either been too subtle or he wasn't that into her.

"Want to talk about it?" he asked.

She pretended to misunderstand, which really, wasn't that difficult. He'd been thoughtful all evening. He could be staring at her for any number of reasons. She had no idea what was going on between them right now. "The plot is nonexistent and the actors don't appear invested. I doubt if it'll launch any careers or win major awards."

"I mean about this." He picked up the remote with his finger and thumb, waggling it in front of her face. "Sorry, but you don't get to hand off responsibility. I'm not into conquests."

She wasn't used to being one. Or making them either. "But you do like the thrill of the hunt."

"In my line of work I kind of have to enjoy it," he agreed. His slow grin had her heart pounding at her ribs. "But when it comes to women, I'm more of a catch-and-release kind of guy."

She gave up trying to play a game she had no hope of winning. "I never know what you're talking about," she confessed. "I wish you'd be more direct."

"Direct, huh?" He studied her for a long moment that quickly became uncomfortable. "Why is it so hard for you to believe I find you beautiful? And that I want to take you to bed?"

The compliment, combined with the heat in his eyes, curled through her. "I have no idea how you find me. We've only known each other a few days."

She didn't know the real him either. He pretended to be so good natured and easygoing. Today she'd seen evidence to the contrary. And she couldn't quite come to terms with how he made her feel. The thought of his hands on her skin stole her breath.

"You've never met a man you've been instantly attracted to?" he asked.

"Of course I have." The proof was sitting beside her.

He flicked off the television and leaned forward to toss the remote on the coffee table. The room plunged into semi-darkness, illuminated only by the single streetlight situated a few yards down the road from the foot of the driveway. The curtains at the floor-to-ceiling windows were drawn back. He slid his arm along the back of the sofa. She'd showered before the movie started, leaving her hair free to dry. His fingers tangled in it at the nape of her neck, tugging through the snarl of loose, slightly damp curls.

"I think we're both clear on what I'm interested in," he said. "My concern is that neither of us knows what you really want, although whatever it is, I'm pretty sure it's nothing short-term."

Short-term was exactly what she wanted from him. The thought of anything else was too ridiculous. And overwhelming. "You think you know me that well after a few phony kisses and a day at the beach?"

"I'm saying you'd never go through with it. You're too…"

His voice trailed off as if he'd thought better of whatever he'd intended to say. His expression, however, made his point loud and clear.

"Boring?" she suggested.

"I thought we'd cleared up that misconception last night. Boring is the last thing I find you. You aren't, however, the kind of girl a guy picks up in a bar for one night."

She crinkled her nose. "I'm judging you right now."

He laughed. "Let me rephrase that. You're more the kind of girl a guy takes home to his mother. I haven't introduced mine to anyone since Sarah Keddy in fifth grade."

Which brought them right back to boring. "Still judging you. For what it's worth, I'm more interested in competing with the kind of woman you'd pick up in a bar than a fifth grader." She drew air into her lungs and went for brave. She swung her leg over his and straddled his hips, resting her palms on his chest. She leaned in close, her lips suspended above his. "I am *very* interested in that one night you speak of. Strictly for research purposes, of course. To see how you'd perform against a baseline."

She read the astonishment in his eyes. Then, the spark of pure lust.

One broad palm cupped the arch of her bottom. Heat scorched through the thin cotton-latex blend of her yoga pants. "I confess I'm a little turned on by the dirty research talk."

"Maybe a discussion on safe sex should come first. I'm

clean and I'm on the pill." She blurted it all out on a single breath, the words tripping over each other.

"Same here, Dr. Babe. Except for the pill part. I'm waiting for you science types to perfect one for men. When you do I'll be all over it. Until then I can probably scrounge up a condom or two if you don't trust me."

"I trust you." She wouldn't be sitting on his lap if she didn't. The last reservations inside her broke free. "I'm still not sure I like being called Dr. Babe though."

"How about if I say it like this?" His fingers eased under the hem of her tank top, caressing the bare flesh of her stomach as they worked their way beneath her bra. She caught her breath, the erotic sensation of his fingertips stroking the sensitive skin beneath the curve of her breast shooting fire to the insides of her thighs. "You are so freaking *hot*, Dr. Babe. I can't wait to be inside you." The evidence of that declaration was apparent, his erection hard and enormous beneath her. His eyes narrowed to cat-like slits in the darkness, predatory, intent, and a total turn on. "Tell me what you'd like me to do to you to get me there."

Talk during foreplay wasn't something she'd ever been good at. Tonight was about seizing opportunities, however, so she was willing to give it a good try, even though her cheeks blazed at the mere thought of it. She caught the lobe of his ear in her teeth and gave it a light nip, then whispered, "I want you to touch me. Lower."

The pad of his thumb swiped across the tip of her nipple. Flames licked at her core. "You can do better than that. Be more specific. Talk dirty to me, babe. Since you're conducting scientific research, if it makes you more comfortable you can even use the right terminology."

Under normal circumstances she would have died of

embarrassment right about now. The few men she'd been with had been more focused on the summation than the preamble. This, however, was Kale. Embarrassment didn't appear to be part of his vocabulary. Not to mention she was already damp from wanting him inside her, and the fastest way to get him there was to cooperate. She didn't intend to be too fast about it however. Proper research took time and the right preparation.

She made a move to roll off his lap. "We should close the curtains."

He held her in place with one hand on her knee. "Learn to relax, Irina. Let go of those inhibitions. It's dark in here and your house is well off the road. No one can see us."

"Someone took photos of me," she reminded him. "That's why you're here."

"I've taken a walk around your house for three nights in a row now and seen no signs of anyone," he assured her. His thumb stroked the inside of her thigh in a silent challenge. "Where's your sense of adventure? But if it makes you feel better…"

The idea of some low-risk exhibitionism was oddly exciting, and definitely outside her comfort zone. She settled back on his thighs. If she planned to do this she'd have to trust him. If they were setting inhibitions free though, then he could go first.

"Take off your clothes," she commanded, to see if he would.

"So that's how it's going to be." Without hesitation, he shrugged out of his T-shirt and tossed it onto the floor. "I say we take turns undressing, but fair warning. There's going to be talking and touching involved. And it'll be dirty."

She inched forward, the apex of her thighs rubbing the

base of his erection. "Let's make sure we have the rules straight. I get to talk and touch first."

"Those are good rules." He leaned back against the sofa. "Be my guest. Why don't we say three of each, talking and touching, per turn? There should be at least one compliment involved in the talking, though."

"Fair enough. Put your hands behind your head."

He complied, lacing his fingers together. "Don't forget the compliment."

"Shh. It's my turn to talk." All her worries over tonight now seemed ridiculous. She could relax and enjoy. Try something new. She tapped her chin with her finger. There'd be no shocking him. He'd made that perfectly clear. Besides, after his investigation was finished, they were never going to see each other again. She could say or do what she liked. "I plan to start at the top and work my way down. *All* the way down."

The thought of how he would taste had her shifting her weight in eager anticipation.

He let out a groan. "Did I say three of each? I meant just one. Either or. And there should be a time limit."

"It's too late to change the rules now." She molded against him, her chest pressed to his, hands on his shoulders, and took his lower lip between her teeth. She drew it into her mouth, nipping and sucking, licking it with the tip of her tongue. She felt the rapid rise and fall of his chest and the quickening pace of his breaths. "I love the shape of your mouth. I can already imagine how good it will feel on my *labia minora*."

"I can't believe you managed to make paying me a compliment sound smart *and* dirty," he growled.

She smiled, ridiculously pleased with herself. She eased back a little, sliding her palms from his shoulders to the heavy pectoral muscles, weighing their solid strength, then lowered her mouth to one of his nipples. She flicked her tongue across it. His back arched in response and he muttered a swear word. She took the dampened flesh between her thumb and forefinger and teased it gently as she moved her tongue to the other nipple.

"This counts as three touches," he warned her, his voice husky. "You've got one comment left. Then it's my turn. Brace yourself."

"That sounds like a promise."

"Oh, it definitely is."

She straightened, trying to think through the puddle her brain had become. "The feel of your hard penis against me makes me wet inside."

Laughter rumbled through his whole body, spreading to hers. "I don't care how scientific I said you could be. I've got to draw the line somewhere. You can't say penis. There's no way I believe it makes you wet when it's making me shrivel, and that's not going to be good for either one of us. Try saying 'dick' for me. Even 'junk' would be better."

His laugh was infectious and tempting, seductive all on its own. She was not, however, changing the script. He'd issued a challenge.

Challenge accepted.

She spread her palms on his rock-solid abdomen, hooking her thumbs in the waistband of his shorts. "What really makes me wet is knowing that as soon as these come off, I'm going to find out how good your penis tastes. I'm going to run my tongue around the rim of your penis and take it into my mouth. I'm going to suck on your penis until you're ready to explode." She eased her hand inside his shorts. He was full and hard. Not at all shriveled. She slid her fingers up and down, then kissed his mouth. "*Penis*," she whispered against his lips for good measure, feeling both wicked and daring.

His laughter choked off. She'd managed to shock him, and herself too, but in a good way. This was so much more fun than she'd expected. She'd never been this turned on by a man in her life. Knowing this was going nowhere—that they'd never meet at a conference, or work on a project together—was liberating in a way she hadn't expected.

He swallowed. "I changed my mind. You can say it as much as you like. But we might have to save that for next time. I'm ready to explode as we speak. Now lose the shirt. It's my turn."

She peeled it off, taking her time.

"Holy crap. *That's* what weapons systems placement designers wear under their clothes?"

Pretty, frilly underwear had always been a weakness of hers. The sexy lingerie gave her more confidence in unfamiliar situations, and Kale, so overwhelmingly male, was about as foreign as anything she'd ever experienced. It was a psychological advantage. But that didn't change the fact that it worked. His reaction proved the effect wasn't only on her.

She tossed her tank top to the floor. "Want to see what else we wear under them?"

"Do I ever." He crooked a finger under the clasp at the front. "I want you to strip for me."

He was testing her. Seeing how far she'd go. Dirty talk, it seemed, wasn't going to be enough. It wasn't for her either. Tonight she planned to be bold.

She pushed off his thighs and stood so she faced him. He stretched his legs out, his erection straining the front of his shorts, his eyes heavy on her as he settled back to watch. She half turned away and undid the clasp of her bra, then slid the straps off her shoulders, one at a time, covering her breasts with an arm. She dropped the bra to the floor and faced him again, cupping her breasts in her hands, inching her fingers apart so her nipples peeped through. Slowly, she lowered her hands.

"You are so fu—freaking beautiful," he said. "I want to suck on them both. I want to take your sweet ass in my hands and I want to pound my dick in you so hard, you'll scream my name when you come."

She tilted her head and looked him up and down. "You think you can make me scream?"

"Baby, I know I can."

She wriggled out of the yoga pants and kicked them aside. She watched his jaw drop at the sight of the thin scrap of pink thong they'd been hiding. She traced a fingertip over the tiny triangle of lace at the front, then nudged her finger underneath it to touch herself in a way she would never have dreamed of doing with anyone else. He wasn't walking away from her tomorrow thinking she was a prude.

"This," she said in the same prim, scholarly tone she'd use at a lecture while fondling her mound with a sweep of her thumb, "is called a *mons veneris*. It's all yours if you want it."

"I do. And I think I'll unwrap it myself. It's time I did some touching."

He caught her hips with his hands and drew her toward him until he had her trapped between his thighs. The coarse blond hairs on his legs rubbed against her skin, already sensitive with anticipation. He hooked his thumb in the strings of her thong and slid the panties out of the way. He eased a finger into her damp folds, stroking until he had her breathless.

"Oh my God." Irina grabbed his shoulders to steady herself. She closed her eyes. Heat scorched through her frame, leaving her trembling with need. "More. I want more."

His smile was one of pure, male self-satisfaction. "That's not my name. Let's hear you say it."

"Kale." She clutched him tighter. His finger moved in and out. Any second now she was going to orgasm. She bit her lip, trying to hold back.

"Louder."

"*Kale.*"

"And what do you want from me?"

She opened her eyes and met his in the semidarkness. "I want you to make me scream."

He took his hand away, skimming out of his shorts and lifting her onto his lap. She fisted his shaft, guiding the tip of his erection into position, stroking her thumb under the velvety rim. His hips bucked upward. He began sliding into her, inch by slow inch, hot and hard and thick. She sucked in a sharp breath, afraid she might pass out from the pleasure of it.

Instantly, he stopped. His hands braced her, supporting her weight on his forearms, his fingers digging into her buttocks. "You OK? Because this has got to be good for us both, not just me."

Having sex with a giant had its drawbacks. Physically she only had as much control as he gave her, and right now she did *not* want him to stop.

"Oh, it's good," she assured him. "And if you'll let me do things my way, it will get even better."

"Big talk, Dr. Babe," he teased, easing his full length inside her. His thumbs roamed her belly, trailing fire in their wake.

"Are you disappointed so far?" she panted, more intent now on actions than words. She rose on her knees ever so slightly, then settled again, taking him deeper. Her inner muscles clenched, adjusting to the feel and the fit of him.

His eyes glittered at her in the darkness. "Not even a little."

He thrust upward, again, then again, establishing a rhythm until she shuddered, unable to hold back any longer. She cried out as her orgasm ripped through her. He arched his back, lifting his hips off the sofa. His hands slid to her breasts and he groaned as he spilled inside her.

She collapsed on his chest with them still connected, limp with spent pleasure and more satisfied than she could have believed possible. They were both breathing hard. She could feel his heart pounding, and the rise and fall of his rib cage beneath her. The world settled back into place.

If this was what being brave and talking dirty earned her, then she was all for it.

"That," Kale said slowly, the husky, raw words rolling over her head in the darkness, "was an experiment that bears repeating." The rough pads of his fingertips mapped the length of her spine, a languorous and sensual caress that had her shivering with rekindled need within seconds. His voice deepened. "I believe I owe you a few compliments, Dr. Babe."

CHAPTER SEVEN

BEST NIGHT OF HIS life.

The spare bedroom was gloomy in the gray light of dawn. A light rainfall pattered against the steel roof and on the ground outside the open window. They'd stumbled into his room after the first round of sex, with him carrying her in his arms and her legs wrapped around his waist.

He watched her face as she slept, nestled against him in a double bed that was far too small for a man of his size, but right now suited him perfectly. She had one bare leg pressed between his thighs. Her hand was trapped against his ribs by the weight of his arm, her fingers curled into a tiny ball. She was using the crook of his elbow as a pillow and he could feel her breath against his throat every time she exhaled.

He snagged a damp tendril of hair off her face with the tip of a finger. She murmured in her sleep, her freckled nose crinkling as it did whenever she was irritated, in a way that made her look so freaking pretty. She snuggled in closer, all naked and warm. Her dark lashes fluttered but she didn't wake. She felt like a priceless piece of art in his arms. He was afraid if he moved she might break, although she'd already proved that was unlikely to happen.

He would never have believed the woman he'd first met—the Dr. Glasov who'd been so uptight and nervous around him—could turn out to be so broad-minded and demanding in bed. She'd been tentative at first, true enough, but as soon as she'd figured out he'd go along with whatever she wanted without being judgy, she'd turned into someone different entirely.

And the dirty talk... Another total surprise. He'd never have imagined a clinical recitation of body parts could be so erotic. Having it come from the mouth of a well-educated pixie made it that much more of a rush.

However, one thing about her hadn't changed despite all the intimate things that they'd done together—or maybe because of them. Ultimately, sweet, pretty Irina Glasov was no one-night stand. He should be ashamed of himself for sleeping with her. Part of him was. Unfortunately, the part controlling his brain where she was concerned had no discernible conscience, because it said he'd do it all over again. Just the thought of her mouth on him had him hard.

He should also drag his ass out of bed and take another walk around her property and at least pretend to be doing his job. It would give him a chance to clear his head too. But she had a tendency to overthink everything. Did he want to risk her waking up in bed alone and getting the wrong idea about what last night had been?

What idea, exactly, did he want her to get?

Now he was the one overthinking the whole situation. She was direct. That was one of the reasons he found her so appealing. He'd make her breakfast again. After that they could talk. She was smart. Another reason he liked her. She'd understand that his work had to come first, and why he had no room in his life for a relationship. The altercation at the beach yesterday had reinforced that for him. He wasn't introducing Irina into his world. A few pop-ups were nothing compared to the potential threats his work might bring down on her, and he simply wasn't the kind of man who could trust her safety to others.

She stretched, rolling to her back and out of his arms. She raised her elbows over her head and stretched as she opened her eyes. She cast him a slow, sleepy smile.

"Wow," she said. "You're even gorgeous first thing in the morning. How is that fair?"

That smile turned his insides to mush. "You're one to talk, beautiful." He bent his head for a kiss. "Besides, it isn't quite morning. The sun isn't up."

"What would you like to do until then?"

He had a list. It started with tasting the rosy tip of the breast peeking at him from above cream-colored sheets. Then he'd work his way down her smooth skin and that flat length of belly. He dragged his attention back to her eyes, all slumberous and sexy. There was no mistaking what she had on her mind.

A tickle of wind stirred the curtains at the window. "We should probably discuss a few things first."

He couldn't believe he'd just said that.

Neither, apparently, could she. "You mean right *now*?"

His timing was so, so bad. He should have waited a half hour before starting this conversation. His conscience, however, had finally caught up with him. Boundaries needed to be set. He couldn't take this any further without making sure she understood where it was headed. She deserved so much better from him.

Now that he'd started it, however, he didn't know what to say next.

"If this is the requisite 'Let's keep things friendly,

we're here for a good time,' speech, then there's no need
to bother," she said before he could pull his own thoughts
into order. "We lead completely different lives. We both
already know this isn't going anywhere. Why not just
enjoy it while it lasts?"

At first he couldn't figure out what the hell she was
talking about. Then it finally clicked. He was the one
getting the 'morning after' speech. And a few things
began to make sense. They'd had sex on her sofa. They'd
used his room, not hers, for the rest of the night. She was
keeping things between them as impersonal as possible
given all that they'd done, and considering she'd cried his
name out. Twice. So he couldn't put his finger on why he
felt so insulted. She was offering him what he'd said he
wanted.

Or she might be playing some game of her own. She
was a woman. And she was smart.

Then again, it wasn't as if an intelligence officer was
some great catch for a woman with a couple of masters
degrees, a PhD, and a career way more impressive than
his.

"When are you going to report the botnet?" she was
asking.

"The what?" He couldn't keep up. His head was in two
different places. It didn't help that her bare toes were
tickling the back of his calf.

She wrapped a strand of his hair around her finger and
tugged on it, reclaiming his attention, drawing his face
closer to hers. "Last night? The RBN?"

Oh. That. "I'll do it this morning."

He'd call Dan at home on his personal line and find out
what the next move should be. He doubted if anything
would change. Internet security was an issue for their
counterpart, CSEC, but no intel was getting passed on to

other departments until the director approved it. The botnet intrusion had come in on her personal computer, not her work one, and she swore she didn't keep anything sensitive on it, so national security wasn't an issue.

On the other hand, CSIS had an interest in Irina and there was enough going on with her to warrant his sticking around.

He wasn't quite ready to give up whatever this was they had going on between them either, regardless of what her game might be.

She disengaged herself from his arms and legs and slid from his bed, her tousled hair an adorable, tangled mess around her shoulders, her bare skin a warm, pearly glow in the watery light. She looked at the floor, but if she was searching for her clothes, they were spread all over the living room where they'd tossed them last night. He'd love to hear her say penis again, but suspected he'd already ruined any possibility of that happening right now. He needed to learn to keep his big mouth shut. This was why he stayed away from nice girls.

"Where are you going?" he asked, holding out hope.

"Last night was fun, but since I'm awake already, I've got to get some work done today." She crooked her hair behind her ear, all curvy hips, slender legs, and perky breasts. "It's my turn to cook breakfast too."

She sauntered from the bedroom, those bare, sexy hips swaying, leaving the door open behind her. He remembered how her pink thong looked, nestled between those firm round cheeks, and his groin shot him a reprimand for the cold shower in the morning forecast.

He rolled to his back and folded his arms behind his head. He heard the door to her bedroom close, the latch making a loud and definitive click. He got the message. Her room was off-limits.

Well, they'd established those boundaries they needed. And he didn't like them.

While Irina cooked breakfast, Kale got dressed. Rain continued to fall, steady but not hard, and the weather was warm so that was no excuse to keep him inside. He'd take a quick look around, then make that phone call to Ottawa he'd promised her.

She had a nice piece of property, private but not too secluded, with a tidy back yard and a patio off the kitchen, even though he didn't like that it was surrounded by trees. He'd searched them more than once but the hordes of bloodthirsty mosquitoes made it an unlikely location for anyone to set up surveillance. He'd concentrated more on the road out in front where the original photos appeared to have been taken.

The rain had mellowed the mosquitoes this morning so he decided to take a more thorough trek through the bushes. He stepped over bushy ferns and around fallen tree trunks, the ground mulchy and soft. Water dripped from the branches and leaves overhead. It wasn't long before his jeans and shirt were soaked through and his shoes were sopping so that he slogged with each step.

Nobody in their right mind would be hiding in this swamp. There were easier ways for a peeping Tom to keep an eye on Irina.

As he turned to head back to the house he glanced up and took a good look through the branches. A tiny black shadow, out of place against the gray-white trunk of a birch, caught his attention. He stood beneath the tree and stared into the thick mass of foliage above his head. The sky was almost completely obliterated. The view of the house, however, was not.

His chest constricted. Someone had set up a surveillance camera and it was trained on Irina's front window. His own words, so cocky and confident, came back to haunt him.

Learn to relax, Irina. Let go of those inhibitions.

The things they'd done. That he'd talked her into doing...

His first angry instinct was to climb the tree, tear down the camera, and smash it to pieces. His second, more professional, reaction was to leave it right where it was. If the camera was digital and had its video rolling twenty-four/seven, the damage was already done. The best thing to do was wait and see what images turned up where— and better yet, who might come back to retrieve their equipment.

But what was best sure as hell didn't feel right.

He owned this disaster. He'd really thought some geeky guy with more brains than common sense was behind those photos of her. As a result he hadn't taken her concerns seriously enough. When combined with the online harassment, and the trail to the RBN, this was some serious shit.

That still didn't make it a matter for CSIS. She didn't work at home on the project that had sparked their interest in her. She kept it isolated on a dedicated computer. Everything in that respect was secure.

Somehow, he doubted if any of that was going to make her feel better about this. She'd trusted him and he'd let her down, and in the worst way imaginable. She was going to kill him when she found out. He couldn't blame her.

He trudged through the trees and shrubs to the house,

his stomach tied in tight little knots. Instead of going inside he leaned against the far end of the brick bungalow so that he was partially out of the rain. From there he called his team leader. He didn't dare chance having Irina overhear this particular conversation.

"It's 8:27 on a Sunday morning," Dan barked when he answered. "This had better be good."

"I'd like to preface this conversation by reminding you that officially, I'm on vacation," Kale said.

There was a long stretch of silence. "Tell me this doesn't involve criminal charges against you."

Kale filled him in. When he was done he could hear Dan taking deep breaths on the other end of the line. That wasn't good.

"I am so pissed off right now I don't even know where to begin. What part of 'Dr. Glasov is important' did you not understand?"

He went with the only defense he could think of and it wasn't great. "I thought it was her work CSIS was interested in."

"It is. But if she's got it all on a dedicated and secure computer, where do you suppose someone might go to get at the information they *can* access? Why do you think someone might be trying to intimidate her?"

Cold sweat mingled with the rain dripping down the back of Kale's neck. "Is she in danger?"

"How the hell should I know? You're the one watching her. When you aren't fucking her, that is."

When Dan started swearing it meant things were bad. Very bad. "What do I tell her?"

"You tell her nothing. We don't want to tip anyone off that we found that camera." There was a bit of a pause, as if Dan were trying to decide how much to reveal. "Someone in the government is stealing Canadian weapons systems parts. Now it looks like they're going after sensitive defense information too. And this is the second connection to the RBN that I've heard about. Do you think you can convince her to go a little bit deeper?"

"You mean get her to hack into the RBN? I'd say the chances of that happening are slim. She wouldn't do it last night."

She knew as well as they did that the RBN had connections to the Russian Mafia. If she still had family there they'd be vulnerable. He had no idea how close she might be to them, or how she'd feel if they were threatened because of something she'd done.

"We need to figure out who's behind those military thefts. And if they're tied to Dr. Glasov somehow. The fear here in Ottawa is that the RBN connection goes pretty high up the food chain." Meaning straight to a minister's office. "We're trying to keep that piece of intelligence contained." Kale could almost hear the wheels spinning as Dan sifted through everything on the other end of the line, assessing the potential complications. "About that other thing… If video footage of the two of you doing the nasty does show up, whether he likes it or not, the director might have to go to CSEC for help to keep it from spreading around the Internet. If that exacerbates his current problems you're going to hear about it. There's a strong possibility Dr. Glasov can do as much by way of containment as CSEC can, though. She'd have the greatest incentive to keep it private."

Kale closed his eyes. "She says cybersecurity isn't her area."

"That doesn't mean she's not as good as, or better than, whoever set up that camera."

He hoped Dan was right. The botnet trail she'd

followed last night had taken her hours. She'd said it was professional.

He also hoped not telling her about the camera was the right thing to do. He did know it was the option he preferred, because right now he was very afraid of how she'd react. With a little luck it hadn't recorded anything and he was worrying for nothing.

"Do everyone a favor and keep your dick on a leash from now on," Dan advised him. "I like it better when I have to handle complaints about you fighting. Jesus." He hung up.

Kale slid his phone into his pocket. He thumped the back of his head against the brick wall. Last night might have been amazing, but this morning blew chunks.

Irina shut off her computer and rolled her chair away from her desk. Her office window overlooked the parking lot. She could her car four stories below, not far from the commissionaire's station, and knew Kale would be patiently waiting for her, observing everyone who came and went from the building.

For the past two days she'd made him wait an extra two hours out of spite.

Even though three full days had passed, and they were now well into their fourth, she continued to fume. He'd told her very little about the report on the botnet he'd made to Ottawa, only that he'd spoken to someone and he was to continue to stay close to her. Those instructions, apparently, didn't include spending any more nights with them naked.

She might have pretended to be OK with him starting

Sunday morning off suffering regrets from the night before, but in reality, she wasn't. Being his one-night stand she could handle. The sex had been good. Incredible, in fact. She'd gotten the distinct impression he'd thought it was too. But did she come across as so desperate that he immediately assumed one night of great sex with him meant she expected some sort of commitment?

How offensive was *that*?

Tonight she had no plans to stay late at the office simply so she could avoid him. Even she had her limits when it came to how much she worked and her brain needed a break. Cooking was her way to decompress.

She gathered her purse and her laptop, locked the office door behind her, and made a mad dash for the elevator, the heels of her shoes clicking like machine-gun fire against the tiled floor. She squeezed between the gleaming doors a split second before they slid shut.

The department's administrative assistant, a pretty blond girl named Christine, sporting a high ponytail and the smoothest complexion Irina had ever seen, was the only other occupant.

She smiled at Irina.

"Hi, Dr. Glasov. Can I add you to the list of people going bowling Friday night?" Irina's confusion must have shown on her face. "The retirement party for Tim Bailey?" the girl prompted. "I need to order the pizza."

Tim Bailey was one of the company's mail deliverymen, and hugely popular with staff throughout the company, and no, Irina hadn't really been planning to go. Pizza and bowling weren't really her thing. She started to give her regrets when she had a much better idea. Regardless of how annoyed she was with Kale right now, he had a job to do. The sooner he did it the faster he'd be out of her house. This was an opportunity for him to meet the people from her workplace without being too obvious about it.

"Would Tim mind if I brought a date?"

Christine's cheeks dimpled. "Not if your date's a good bowler."

Irina couldn't say for certain whether he was or not, but she'd be surprised if the answer was no. Kale Martin did everything well. Except, it would seem, mornings after.

"I can guarantee he'll be better than me. I haven't bowled since I was eleven or twelve."

Kale was out of the car and walking toward her, god-like and golden, the personification of Thor, the second he saw her exit the building. She had a sudden and very vivid recollection of how he'd looked naked.

How he'd *felt*.

"*That's* your boyfriend?" Christine asked, wide-eyed with respect. "Is he a model?"

"Surfer," Irina contradicted her. "I know. He's pretty, right?" Then she remembered to stick to their cover story. "Actually, he's a teacher."

"I bet his detentions are totally worth it."

Christine stayed by Irina's elbow, clearly expecting an introduction. She was very pretty and Kale was a flirt. Irina wondered how he'd react.

With indifference, as it turned out.

"Hey, babe," he said to Irina. "How was your day?" He took her bag from her, as considerate as always, but they had an audience today so he bent his head and kissed her, too. He seemed more willing to get into character in public where it was safe.

Three nights of frustration simmered inside her. It was possible his libido wasn't as active as hers, but she didn't buy it. Neither, however, could she explain his sudden and complete lack of physical interest in her. She could think of nothing she'd done wrong—meaning she'd spent far too much time analyzing events.

She came to a decision. No more overthinking. She wasn't used to all this angry frustration. He didn't have to sleep with her again if he didn't want to, but he didn't get to make her feel cheap about it either. If she was a one-night stand, then he was a dog. She leaned into the kiss, rising on her toes as she slipped her fingers into the base of that delectable man bun. She ran her tongue across the seam of his lips. He wasn't the only one who could play to the crowd.

His eyes, locked on her face, filled with rueful amusement as they pulled apart. He knew what she was trying to do. But she also detected a satisfying level of smoldering heat. The attraction was still there. So what was his problem?

She'd almost forgotten Christine, who was watching their interaction with blatant interest, unable to mask her disbelief as her bright gaze shifted between them. Irina could well imagine what she was thinking. What on earth could a man as gorgeous as Kale see in the studious and dull Dr. Glasov?

She made the introductions.

Christine offered Kale her hand and it disappeared inside his much larger fist. Her dimples flashed. "Pleased to meet you. Dr. Glasov signed you both up for bowling Friday night, so I guess we'll meet again."

"She did, did she?" Blue eyes again fixed on Irina. Dark blond eyebrows lifted. "Aren't you full of surprises?"

And wasn't he full of—

He made that sound so suggestive. Her temper spiked again. She wrestled it under control. Kale Martin pushed every last button she owned simply by being himself.

"I had no idea you bowled," he said once they were inside the car.

"I don't. But it gives you a chance to meet a few of the people I work with." She told him about the retirement party.

He turned the air conditioning to high. Cold air shot from the dash. "I thought it was written somewhere that computer geeks are crappy at sports? How likely is it that anyone even close to your level in the company will be there?"

"I have no idea," she had to admit. "But for your information I went to university with an Olympic swimmer and she graduated third in our class, so I think that stereotype's been disproven. Besides, bowling isn't a real sport."

"If you want to get invited again you should probably keep that opinion to yourself. Serious bowlers can be touchy."

"I'll take my chances. I don't really see myself becoming a regular."

He pulled up to the last set of lights before they turned onto the highway, tapping his thumbs on the steering wheel as they waited for them to change. The light shifted to green and the car surged forward, merging into a steady stream of afternoon traffic.

"Can we make a quick stop at the grocery store?" she asked. "I want to pick up a few things for dinner."

"I took care of that already. I've got a casserole warming in the oven."

So much for decompressing this evening. Now she had nothing but work to distract her. The evening promised to be long and uncomfortable. She should have stayed at the office.

Fifteen minutes later, they were home.

The smell of fresh-cut grass greeted her as she stepped from the car. He'd mowed her lawn and tackled the jungle of overgrowth around the border of her property. A tangle of brush had been neatly stacked in one corner of her yard.

"You didn't need to do that," she said when she saw it, at a loss for words. "But thank you," she hastily added.

"I've been bored out of my mind." She didn't quite know how to take that and he must have sensed it. A slight smile touched his lips as if he knew where her thoughts had headed. "With my own company," he added. "Your reading material is over my head. Besides." He closed the car door and rested his arms on the roof as he spoke to her across it. "I need to be doing something physical in my downtime. Maybe tomorrow I'll head to the beach."

"You shouldn't go surfing alone." Her response was automatic. Her disapproval, difficult to hide. He was far too cocky and self-assured for his own good.

"I've been surfing alone since I was eleven. And it's really doubtful the beach will be empty. But thank you for your concern." He continued to watch her over the roof of the car. He looked as if he had something more he wanted to say, then thought better of it.

Irina headed for the house before she blurted out what she had on her mind instead. She might not have a whole lot of experience with men like him, but she wasn't completely naïve. She didn't believe he was no longer interested in her. Not when he looked at her in a way that shot bolts of electricity straight to her *mons veneris*.

Something had to be wrong.

Maybe she should be worried, not angry.

Dinner was quiet. After the table was cleared and the

dishes were done he prowled restlessly around the house, no longer as easygoing as he'd seemed to be at first. This was like being trapped with a caged lion. He made her nervous too.

He stopped at the living room window, peering out from behind the long length of flowered drapery. He let the fabric drop into place. "What do you do for fun in the evenings when I'm not around? Please don't tell me you work every night."

He wasn't normally like this. If she hadn't been so focused on sex she would have seen it before. She should definitely be worried. She still wasn't sure that sex wasn't the problem though, so she didn't dare come right out and ask what was wrong. No matter what was the root cause of his restlessness, he was going to deny it existed.

"What do you usually do?" she countered, unwilling to admit out loud that yes, she did work most of the time. She was a scholar. A scientist. As well as the upcoming conference, she had a new book she was contracted to write. Cooking was her only real hobby.

"I don't keep normal hours. When I'm free I go out in the evenings. To bars. Concerts. Sometimes the gym." His eyes lit up. "Change into jeans and anything but high heels, Dr. Babe," he said. "Preferably sneakers if you've got them. We're going out."

CHAPTER EIGHT

"I DON'T KNOW ABOUT this."

Irina stared at the climbing wall. It was a long way to the top. Colorful hand and footholds had been bolted from floor to ceiling, but anything that required signing a personal disclaimer couldn't be safe.

"Don't worry so much. You'll give yourself wrinkles." Kale adjusted the harness fastened between her legs and around her hips to his satisfaction, then clipped it to the rope. "The rope is fastened to the floor. You can't fall. And when you're ready to start down, I'll have control of the brake. We can go as slow as you like." He brought his mouth close to her ear so that the warmth of his breath tickled her throat and ratcheted her pulse up a notch. "Do you like it slow?"

Whatever was bothering him, here, in a public place, he was much more relaxed. More like himself—or who she'd thought him to be—and she couldn't figure out why. It was driving her crazy.

She concentrated on rubbing chalk on her hands. "You should pay attention and find out which I prefer."

He straightened. "Don't kid yourself, Dr. Babe. I pay attention. But for now, it's best if we keep the brakes on. You'll just have to trust me on that."

He hadn't cared about brakes Saturday night. He was a risk taker. He'd encouraged her to take a few too. She hadn't been naked alone. Neither had she begged him for a commitment, or assumed it meant anything serious. She'd taken nothing for granted. So what would make him hold back?

When, exactly, had things gone wrong?

The sequence of events clicked into place, from their conversation in bed to his trip outdoors, where he'd made a call to report on the botnet. Her skin flushed hot, then slicked with ice. Her breath froze in her chest.

"Oh my *God*. You told Ottawa that you *slept* with me, didn't you? You...you..." She was too enraged to articulate. She gave him a shove. She might as well have pushed at the wall. Those gorgeous blue eyes expanded, but other than that, he didn't budge.

His face, however, turned a dull red. So did the tips of his ears. "Penis?" he supplied, but he kept his voice low. "This might not be the best place to have this conversation."

Irina, normally the soul of discretion, was beyond caring. It was evening on a weeknight. The gym was mostly empty. Besides the attendant, who was sorting equipment and not paying them any attention, there were only two other people and they were both climbing. One was an obvious expert, moving horizontally along the wall just beneath the ceiling, well over their heads. The other was on the opposite side of the large room, inside a cave-like structure, climbing without a harness above a giant mattress. "Why not? Nobody's listening."

"There are ears everywhere. Take it from me."

She'd known his job was to gather intelligence. It was her fault for thinking the intelligence gathering would stop at the bedroom door. She took a few deep, shaky breaths that didn't help. "Get this harness off me. I want to go home. *Now*."

He caught her hands as she tugged at the straps, trying to loosen them. He bent his knees and brought his face close to hers, peering into her eyes. "Has it occurred to you that maybe I've been under considerable stress the past few days and need to work some of it off, and that my preferred method might be off-limits?"

His voice curled around her. She bit the inside of her lip to keep it from trembling with rage. How dare he try to placate her by referring to Saturday night? How much stress did he think she'd been under?

Her own words were icy. "Has it occurred to *you* that the details of your 'preferred method' include me, and will be going into a file where people check my security clearances?"

He squeezed her fingers. "Nothing that happened between us is going into any file."

Despite her common sense telling her she was crazy for it, she wanted to believe him. "Then why would you say anything to Ottawa about it in the first place?"

"It's complicated." He straightened, still holding her hands. "My communication with my team leader is based on honesty and complete disclosure. If what happened between you and I should ever take on relevance at some point down the road, and I hadn't told him about it, then our working relationship would be damaged."

He'd put his career ahead of her privacy. Rather than wanting to kill him for it, which she did, she tried to see it from his point of view. After all, he owed her nothing. She'd simply assumed discretion was part of the deal. This was what she got for sleeping with a virtual stranger. The entire evening had been completely out of character for her. And yet it had been an amazing experience. Disappointment, unwanted, that a repeat was now off the agenda warred with her anger. What helped a little—a *very* little—was finding out he'd spent the past few days frustrated too.

She jerked her hands out of his. If they went home now, the rest of the evening would be spent in awkward and uncomfortable silence—on her part at least. The coming days and nights didn't bear thinking about.

"Fine. Since I'm already harnessed, let's get this over with."

It might not hurt for her to work off some stress too.

That hadn't gone well at all.

Despite the outer sweetness and timidity, and the sensuality she kept well under wraps, Dr. Babe had a temper. Determination to go with it too.

Kale kept one eye on the belaying line, making sure she was safely anchored as she made slow but steady progress up the wall. How far she climbed would be directly proportional to her anger. His money was on her hitting the roof.

He hadn't expected her to figure out what he'd spoken to Dan about, which was dumb on his part. So far, she'd figured out everything. She was going to figure out about that camera too, and being under a direct order not to tell her about it wasn't going to save him. He'd really screwed up and he didn't know how to fix things with her. This was why he didn't date women with brains. Trying to keep a step ahead of them was exhausting.

One of her feet slipped off a rock, leaving her dangling

in midair, legs flailing. She made the mistake of looking at the floor. Panic skittered across her face. "Bring me down!"

No way. She could do this. She simply had to have more confidence in her abilities beyond those attached to her computer. He held the brake steady while he called out reassurance, then instructions. "I've got you. You aren't going to fall. Grab onto the wall and take a few seconds to calm down and catch your breath. Move your left foot a little higher. That's it. Keep your eyes on the wall, not the floor. Once you get your balance back, then you can decide if you want to come down or finish the climb. You don't have much farther to go." She was only a few yards from the top. He hated to see her lose her nerve now. "You can do this."

"My arms are tired."

"That's good," he encouraged her. "You're supposed to be using your upper body the most. But if you've got a good foothold now, rest your weight on your legs and give your arms a break."

She wasn't in any danger. This was an easy climb meant for beginners. It was how she felt, however, that really mattered to him. If she did decide to quit, he wouldn't judge her. It hadn't been her choice of entertainment to come here tonight. Next time he'd have to think of something she would enjoy.

She clung to the wall, pulling herself together. "I'm going to finish," she said, sounding as determined as if she'd decided to crest the summit of Kilimanjaro.

Everything she did, she did with such serious focus it made him smile. He was never going to forget the lesson she'd given him in female anatomy. He'd never look at a clitoris the same way again either.

She made it to the top. A short while later she was

back on the mat beside him. He began unhooking her harness.

"I did it," she said.

The glow of pure pleasure flushing her cheeks punched his brain because he'd seen that expression before, only under much different circumstances. She was so right. He should have kept his mouth shut about them sleeping together. If he had, he could take her in his arms right now and congratulate her the way he wanted. But if a video of that night in her living room should ever turn up, Dan needed to be prepared.

She should be prepared too. There was a very good chance that if he told her about it, however, she'd be afraid, and he'd rather she remained angry. She was a scholar. A researcher. Designing weapons systems placement was nothing more than an intellectual pursuit and a paycheck to her. He doubted reality had ever factored into any of it before. Someone was phishing for information on her computers, and if they couldn't get it one way from her, what would be the next method they tried?

Best not to head down that road.

Not yet.

"You did indeed," he congratulated her. He went to one knee to help her step out of the harness, sliding one hand over her hip, taking unfair advantage of an excuse to touch. He wasn't going to get too many opportunities now that he'd been told to back off.

She stiffened. She gripped his arm to keep from falling over as she lifted her foot. Her fingers tightened. "I'm still angry."

"I know."

He glanced into those sea-green eyes, almost at a level with his. Her pink lips were pressed tight. His heart clenched with regret. She was so freaking adorable. Sleeping in the room next to hers was all kinds of torture. One night hadn't been nearly enough, and it bugged the hell out of him that she'd given him the *This isn't going anywhere so let's just have fun* speech. They'd had more than fun.

He lengthened the straps on the harness so it would fit his bulkier frame. Once everything was secure and he'd fastened himself to the floor, he scouted out which route on the wall he'd take to the top, but he had a lot of other things on his mind too. Most had to do with Irina. He hadn't yet figured out a way to convince her to hack into the RBN. That was going to be a lot more difficult than climbing a wall wearing safety gear.

And a whole lot less fun than getting her naked.

Friday night, they arrived at the bowling alley fashionably late.

Irina'd had difficulty deciding what to wear, obsessing over her appearance for a full forty-five minutes before Kale finally, in desperation, insisted she go casual. She'd settled on a pair of black yoga pants topped with a modest pink cotton T-shirt, and twisted her hair into a knot on top of her head that she secured with an elastic band. While personally he liked it loose best, the result was sloppily sexy, as if she'd just crawled out of bed. Girl problems were hot as hell. He loved them. Another ten minutes and they wouldn't have been leaving the house. He'd have peeled her clothes off, tossed her on her back, and licked that luscious *labia minora* until she screamed out his name. Again and again.

And he wouldn't have cared what Dan might have to say about it either. Dan had obviously never suffered from a five-day erection.

The sounds of balls clattering down the alleys and pins crashing greeted them as they walked through the doors. This was their first real public performance and tonight, he got to touch and tease as much as he liked—within reason of course. It was part of the game. He ran his hand over the small of her back. He'd been trying to figure out what she had on underneath those stretchy pants and that T-shirt since they'd left the house. The distinct lack of panty lines offered his imagination plenty of possibilities.

She was killing him.

She edged away from his hand, going Dr. Glasov on him. "My usual man candy for work functions tends to be more circumspect."

They wouldn't be if they knew of her preference for thongs.

The walls and ceiling were built to deaden sound. While there was little chance they'd be overheard past the racket from the balls and the pins, he really did dislike discussing anything about their working relationship in public. He made his living listening to other people talk and making observations. Their body language, too, was a factor that could give them away. And right now Irina's said volumes. She was nervous, whether of him or the crowd he couldn't be certain. Either way she needed to loosen up.

"If you had a usual man candy it would be bland vanilla. I'm the whipped cream, sprinkles, and cherry on top of your sundae. Now play along," he chided her. "We're a couple, remember?"

"Since I'm playing the gainfully-employed role in this relationship, I'll buy the beer."

She had a quick sense of humor, another well-hidden quality that fascinated him. He watched her cross the promenade to the bar, those curvy hips swaying with an unconscious but very erotic allure, bringing vividly to mind the striptease she'd done for him. It had been…memorable. No one would ever believe it of her.

Not unless it had been caught on camera.

He went to get the bowling shoes. While he waited for the attendant to find their sizes, he checked out the crowd. There had to be easily fifty people from Irina's workplace, although he had no idea how many might belong in her actual department. Most of them had already divided up in teams and were occupying lanes. Since he couldn't imagine Irina insinuating herself into a group of people she didn't know well, he was going to have to decide which one they'd join.

She reappeared with two bottles of beer, squeezing between two men who were standing with their backs together and talking to different people, oblivious to her passage behind them. She popped free, then traded Kale one of the bottles for a pair of shoes.

"That's it for me and beer, babe," he said as they made the exchange. The bottle was a prop. He didn't plan on drinking when he still had concerns for her safety. "I'm the designated driver. You might want to take it easy too," he teased her. "You've already proved you're a lightweight."

She made a face at him and took a healthy swig, just to be contrary. He commandeered a seat on a low wooden bench and kicked off his sneakers. He patted the empty space beside him, indicating for her to sit down. She crowded up next to him, so close they were touching, and he lifted an eyebrow at the sudden about face. She'd spent the week keeping her distance. Only moments ago she'd chastised him for getting too far into character—not that he planned to let that stop him. Teasing her had the added benefit of taking her mind off worrying over how the evening would progress. She thought things to death.

"What happened to circumspect?" he asked.

"I hate things like this," she muttered, her eyes reflecting anxiety. "It's noisy and chaotic, I feel underdressed, and I don't know what's expected of me."

None of this came as any great revelation to him. If not for the fact it really was a work event—for them both—he'd encourage her to have a few more drinks and loosen up.

"You're expected to have fun and mingle with people. Think of it as a networking event without the suits and ties." He nudged her with his shoulder. "And by the way, you look beautiful. As usual. I already told you those clothes are completely appropriate. This isn't the Oscars." He bent his head to whisper in her ear. "Although for what it's worth, I'm expecting an Oscar-winning performance from you."

He tied his shoes, waiting while she dawdled over lacing up hers. He'd already figured out which group they should join. Seven women were having a very good time at lane number five. They ranged in age from early twenties to late fifties. One was Christine, the admin assistant Irina had introduced him to. Two others looked as if they might be serious bowlers. The rest appeared more interested in enjoying themselves. With any luck a few of them were executive assistants. EAs always knew everything that went on in a company.

He took Irina's hand. "We're bowling in lane number five."

The women's reactions ranged from guardedness to speculation and outright surprise as he and Irina approached them.

"Hi, Dr. Glasov. Kale," Christine greeted them, her blond ponytail swinging as she stooped to pick up her ball from the return system. "I'm so glad you both made it."

Irina, cool and polite, slipped immediately into her professional persona. "I hope no one's competitive. I can't guarantee my performance."

Christine's smile faltered. Inside, Kale winced. Irina needed to learn how to separate her two personalities when she was outside of the workplace. The dig at him about her acting abilities, he could admire. That really was clever. But remaining professional didn't mean she had to keep a giant stick up her butt all the time.

He slid an arm around her waist and planted a kiss on her forehead. "Not to worry, babe. I'll help you out with any performance issues you have."

Irina's face reddened and everyone laughed, breaking the ice. They had so many double entendres flying around now, it was anyone's game.

A tall, fiftyish woman with short platinum hair, graceful figure, and a commanding presence shook her head. "I think we'd better put you two on opposite teams. Dr. Glasov will bowl with Christine." She held out her hand to Kale. "Hello, new teammate. I'm Meghan."

Once the introductions were made, and Kale established that Irina was going to be OK on team Christine, he took a seat beside Meghan.

"So how do you and Dr. Glasov know each other?" Meghan asked.

Kale dodged the question by countering with one of his own. "Does everyone here call her Dr. Glasov?"

Meghan's eyes twinkled. She drew in her lips, rolling them over her teeth as if biting back whatever she really wanted to say. "Her reputation at the office is somewhat…formidable."

While Irina was all soft and feminine at home—pink sofas never lied—she did seem hung up on the importance of being Dr. Glasov in public. In his head he ran through all the possible ways he could respond to Meghan's comment that might help make Irina appear less stuffy before deciding to let it go. Rome wasn't built in a day and he wasn't paid to be her social advocate. "Do you work in her department?"

The older woman laughed. "Good lord, no. They put all the smart people in the computer science and systems design department. I work for the executive vice president."

Just as he'd hoped, he'd found his primary source of information. If anyone knew anything about any unusual interest in Irina stemming from inside the company, it would be Meghan. "I'd imagine your EVP hires only the best and the best don't always own IQs that start at 145."

"My IQ, whatever it is, appears to be adequate for everyday function. I'm assuming yours is good too." She slid him a sly, knowing look. "I can't see Dr. Glasov being interested in a man strictly for his...appearance. She'd get bored. Eventually."

We both already know this isn't going anywhere.

Irina's words echoed, emphasizing the uncomfortable amount of truth to Meghan's statement. He shoved it aside. "I don't know about that. I'm awfully pretty. And not to brag, but I'm a pretty good time."

Meghan laughed again. "I'm sure you are. Let's hope you're also a good bowler, handsome. You're up."

Kale had never played candlepin bowling. The ball was small, without any holes, and the fallen pins remained in play. Nevertheless, he acquitted himself reasonably well with a strike and a pair.

Next up after him was Irina. He could let her make the

first few attempts on her own, but what would be the fun in that?

He positioned himself behind her and cupped her hand—the one clenching the ball in a death grip—with his much larger palm. He loved the soft scent of her, a combination of vanilla and a subtle undertone with a little more bite. It summed her up nicely. The sharp inhale of her breath as his fingers danced across her ribs had his own breathing suddenly unsteady.

"Hey! No consorting with the enemy," one of the women on his team protested, although her complaint was good natured. A chorus of agreements from the bench, also all in good fun, backed her up.

He could feel Irina start to tense. Her eyes were fixed straight ahead, on the lane.

"Ignore them, babe," he said. "I know my priorities."

"Are you sure about that?" she murmured.

Her quiet, faintly accusing question and the loads of meaning behind it drew him up short. He wasn't sure about anything anymore. Not when it came to her.

He stepped away from her, his hands in the air. "Ladies, you're absolutely right. There will be no more consorting."

Irina turned out to be the worst bowler ever, sending the first two balls down the gutter and the other women into fits of hysterics.

"I can't take it," Meghan said to Kale, shaking her head. "If you won't consort with her, I'm going to have to." She walked over to Irina and took the ball from her hands. "Honey, try putting more hip into it and a little less hop. The ball's not supposed to bounce off the lane like that."

The other women were quick to offer their advice too. As soon as Irina began to relax, so did Kale. She even looked like she might be enjoying herself.

For his part, he spent the rest of the evening ferreting out information. He got nothing useful from Meghan. No, he didn't have any competition for Dr. Glasov's affections that she was aware of. No, she didn't know what Dr. Glasov was working on, and neither did anyone else—it was top secret. Yes, she made all the travel arrangements for senior management, including Dr. Glasov. No, she had no idea what Dr. Glasov's favorite flower might be, but lilies were usually safe. Roses were too cliché.

The men hovering at the bar weren't a whole lot more help. The company had hired good people who were disinclined to talk about their work with strangers, particularly when the questions involved Irina—or rather, the illustrious Dr. Glasov.

By the end of the night he no longer believed she was being targeted by someone inside the company—or at least the possibility was bumped several slots lower. While he'd hardly met everyone, he'd gotten a reasonable sampling of employees from several departments and at multiple levels of authority within them. She simply wasn't part of any loop. She worked on her own and kept to herself. There were no coworkers to know or be jealous of her successes—exactly as she'd tried to tell him, right from the first.

He had to be on the wrong path.

Frustration ate at him all the way home. He'd given her the keys so she could drive since neither of them had had more than the one beer. It kept her occupied and gave him a chance to think about what to do next. If he didn't get some sort of lead soon he was going to have to step up his fact-finding approach. Unfortunately, he had no idea what more he could do other than continue to observe. Dan had tied his hands as far as the use of any government resources he might otherwise have drawn on. He and Irina were in this alone.

He'd already made a really big mistake over that surveillance camera. She also didn't know that CSIS wasn't openly investigating whoever was cyberstalking her. If she ever found out about either of those things she'd never forgive him. He'd dug himself a hole and any second he could be buried in it.

He began picking apart her earlier comment about his priorities, trying to figure out if she'd meant what he thought—that she was as frustrated as he was and about the same thing. Meghan had said Irina would get bored with someone who couldn't stimulate her mentally as well as physically, or words to that effect. Was that why Irina had been so agreeable to keeping things casual between them? Why she'd gone all Dr. Glasov the morning after? He was good in bed, but otherwise no challenge for her?

He'd love to show her he was more than just a pretty face. Unfortunately, in this instance, he wasn't so sure that he was.

CHAPTER NINE

SHE'D HAD A GOOD time. Much better than she'd hoped for. Irina wasn't sure, however, that Kale had learned anything useful.

She set up her laptop on the kitchen table so she could respond to a few time-sensitive, industry-related emails she hadn't been able to address earlier at the bowling alley because she didn't have access from her phone to the necessary data. She never stored important information in any cloud.

Her laptop was taking too long to load. She stared at it, a sinking sensation that was becoming all-too familiar twisting her stomach.

"I've got a problem," she said.

"What is it?"

Kale had been on the other side of the kitchen, staring into the shadowy backyard through the patio doors. He came to where she was sitting and placed a hand on her shoulder, bringing his cheek close to hers as he bent forward so he, too, could look at the screen.

He couldn't seem to help himself. The man was a toucher.

She forgot everything else. All evening he'd been

friendly and charming, the perfect Norse god to take on a date. The women they'd bowled with had been completely bowled over by him, and why wouldn't they be?

She wasn't immune to him either. Not by a long shot. But she couldn't for the life of her figure out the signals he sent.

She tried to focus on the screen and not the incredible sensation of his thumb absently massaging her tense rhomboid muscle. Oddly enough, his touch settled her stomach and nerves. "The botnet is back, which likely means at least one of my contacts was already infected before I could shut it down and it's spreading through all our personal networks."

"Great. Now we're getting somewhere." She could practically hear him rubbing his hands in his head. The pressure on her rhomboid increased in direct proportion to his enthusiasm.

"In what way?" For her, this wasn't a reason to celebrate.

He kept his eyes on the screen and his hand on her shoulder. "If whoever's behind the botnet is the same person—or people—responsible for your pop-ups at work, then they're looking for specific information. If the botnet is spreading through your contacts it's because you have something in common with at least one of them. I wonder if anyone on your contacts list is having the same pop-up problems you are?"

Her chest muscles tightened. He was shifting the focus of his investigation from her current workplace to her external contacts and that wasn't good. "You don't think the weapons systems design project I'm working on is the real target, do you."

"I'm not dismissing the possibility of it just yet, but I do think you know enough geeky science people around the world that I should have been looking at your broader connections long before now." He tapped a link on the screen. One of the emails popped open. He breathed in and out a few times. His tone conveyed awe. "You *know* this guy?"

"We shared the same advisor in grad school." He was a nuclear physicist currently consulting for NASA, but they'd taken a master's program together when she was seventeen. He'd been twenty-nine and infinitely patient when it came to her shyness over public presentations, helping her to get past it.

Kale canted his head to the side and looked at her as if she were a new species that he couldn't quite comprehend. She'd seen that particular expression on people's faces before and didn't like seeing it on his. It never failed to make her feel like a freak. He was probably relieved his boss had told him that sleeping with her wasn't professional. She couldn't even talk dirty in bed like a normal person.

Her fingers automatically went to the keyboard. "I'll send out a group email to let everyone know they've been infected."

He caught her wrist. "Not just yet. Can you print off a copy of your contacts list for me? I want to fax it to my boss in Ottawa to see if he knows of anything going on in the world that might involve one or more of these people." He shook his head as if unable to contain his disbelief. "This reads like a roster of mad scientists working toward world domination."

Irina was immediately defensive. "None of the scientists I know are mad. They aren't interested in world domination. They're dedicated to research."

Blue eyes sparkled with sudden humor. Dark blond eyebrows shifted upward. "Oh my God, Irina. Do you realize I talked Dr. Glasov—a world renowned computer scientist who has friends in high places at NASA—into doing a striptease for me?"

Heat unfurled at her hairline and prickled her scalp. If she were to draw a picture of him at that moment, she'd place a light bulb over his head. Her defensiveness escalated. She wasn't a robot. She had more going for her than any artificial intelligence. She had emotions. Not to mention physical needs that had gone unmet all week.

"Do you think I'm so caught up in research that I can't make up my own mind about what I want or don't want to do and with whom? That I'm not normally interested in sex, but have to be coerced into it?"

His expression turned cautious, the look of a man approaching a minefield with no hope for retreat. He hooked a chair leg with his foot and twirled it around so he could sit facing her. One arm rested on the table. "Let's get back on track. What I need to figure out is why, out of this list, you were targeted. Or *if* you were the target. Or if you were the *only* target." He tapped the corner of her keyboard. "Can you tell me a little about each of these people?"

She chewed on the inside of her cheek. Kale might come across as funny and kind on the surface, but he was CSIS. He looked for trouble, pinching it off before it became an international concern. Giving these names to him would be the same as offering him an open invitation to invade their private lives. It could potentially damage their careers. She wouldn't wish that on anyone let alone colleagues and friends. CSIS was serious business.

So, however, was the botnet. She didn't see that she had any choice.

She gave him a brief rundown of each individual. The list was a long one.

"I'll send it to you electronically," she said when she was done.

The chair creaked as he shifted his weight. "I'd rather have it in print."

She secured a stray strand of hair that had come free and was tickling her neck, working it back under the elastic with her fingers. "My laptop's already been hacked," she pointed out. "The information is out there in the world. If anyone plans to do something with it, it's too late to worry about it."

"I'd rather fax it to Ottawa, just to be safe."

He thought a fax was more secure? "Safe from what?"

"I mean it will be more user-friendly. Dan's old school. Not everyone's as comfortable with technology as you are, you know. Besides." Kale's eyes lit up again, deepening the blue. "I'd rather not get emails from you right now, what with the whole invasive botnet and RBN thing you've got going on. No offense."

Her suspicion intensified. Although the point was a valid one, he was being deliberately evasive. "What's going on that I don't know about?"

"Nothing." He patted her shoulder. He might as well have patted her head. "Quit analyzing the crap out of everything." He stood and straightened, lifting his arms to put his palms on the ceiling in a full-body stretch that showed off a distracting coastline of darkish blond hair and an ocean of rock-solid abs. "I'm going to watch television until bedtime."

The kitchen expanded without his presence to fill it, becoming a giant, empty cavern with corners that echoed. She tapped the mouse pad with her fingertip. She could try removing the botnet again, but what was the point? It would only come back.

If she really wanted to put an end to whatever was

happening she should do as Kale had asked the first time and hack into the RBN. That, however, could be inviting even more trouble. She wanted nothing to do with organized crime.

She closed the laptop. The quiet murmur of the television from the other room was the only sound other than the gentle hum of the fridge. It was too close to midnight to cook, yet she was too wired to sleep. What frustrated her most—what she found the most frightening—was that she'd done nothing to deserve any of this. She'd done nothing wrong.

Her thoughts returned to Kale, an equally big problem. *I talked Dr. Glasov—a world renowned computer scientist who has friends in high places at NASA—into doing a striptease for me.*

Those words still stung. It was true that she'd had to be encouraged. She'd never have done something like that on her own or with anyone else. She'd never have gone to the beach, or wall-climbing, or bowling tonight either. She wouldn't have joined an intimidating group of women who'd turned out to be a lot of fun, and friendly too. They hadn't cared how many papers she'd published or international panels she'd sat on. They'd gone to a great deal of trouble to make sure she felt part of the group in spite of her lack of common ground.

As for Kale…

He might be able to turn the testosterone on and off, but her hormones didn't work the same way. Everyone at her workplace already assumed they were sleeping together. It was his own fault that his boss knew it for a fact. She didn't see how it would matter to anyone if they continued to do so. The barn door was wide open. The horse had already escaped.

And if he no longer believed her work on the weapons

systems design was the reason behind those pop-ups and the botnet, how long would it be before he took his investigation elsewhere and was gone from her life?

Maybe she should take his advice and stop analyzing everything.

He was slouched on her sofa with his bare feet on the coffee table, the remote in his hand and his wrist resting on his thigh. His eyes were on the television, but she suspected, by the slight frown on his face, that his mind was elsewhere. He'd unfastened and combed out his hair. It touched his wide shoulders in blond waves that she itched to dip her fingers into. His shirt was untucked from his jeans.

He could be a centerfold for hot guys at leisure.

The room was lit by the screen and one lamp. She flicked the lamp off. When he looked up, she reached down and plucked the remote from his grasp. She dangled it from her fingertips. "I believe this is mine."

She hit the off button on the remote and the television went silent. The curtains were open, filling the room with a feeble light that leached all the color.

He didn't move. "You have no idea how much I want to peel off every piece of your clothes and lick every inch of your skin, but I promised I'd keep my attention on my job, not my dick."

She tried hard to sound casual. "So keep your attention on your job. I'll keep mine on your..." She swallowed, forcing the word past her lips. "Dick."

His soft chuckle rolled over her. He swung his feet to the floor and stood. "Stripteases. Talking dirty. I feel like I've corrupted a Catholic schoolgirl."

"I'm older than you are." He was thirty. She was thirty-two.

"That's even worse. I've corrupted Mother Teresa. I'm

going straight to hell." He took her arms in his hands, his thumbs brushing the soft inner flesh. "I thought you were mad at me."

"I was. I am." She bit her lip. "So make me change my mind."

He slid his palms up and down her bare skin, his touch light and his palms scratchy. She tipped her head back so she could see his face. It was a blur in the shadows. She couldn't read his expression.

He half laughed, half sighed. "You have no idea how much I'd love to, babe. But believe it or not, my work is important to me. I've already made one mistake. I don't need to make any more."

"Sleeping with me was a mistake?"

"No, I meant..." He reconsidered whatever he'd been about to say. "It's hard to be objective when all I can think about is how things might affect you. Take tonight for instance. I know you didn't want to give me that list of names, and it was so tempting to give in to what you want rather than go after the information I need. I actually asked myself how else I might get it so that it wouldn't affect you. I can't make decisions that way. My work has to come first."

He was lying to her. She didn't have that kind of importance to him. When they'd woken up in the same bed he'd been about to give her the morning after, *Let's keep things casual* speech, so she'd beaten him to it. He had no problem in getting her to do things she didn't want to either. She'd had fun tonight, yes. Did she like bowling any better now? Not in the least. And all evening long she'd watched him charm other women. He'd manipulated them to get information and shown not a hint of remorse.

So he was lying. He was good at it too. She didn't care

why, not really, although it was nice to know where she stood. He could tell his boss whatever story he liked. It wasn't as if she'd contradict him.

"You aren't working right now. I'm not working either. I came to CSIS, not the other way around. I'm not about to do anything to interfere with your investigation." She inched her fingers under the tail of his shirt. The waistband of his jeans was unfastened. She nudged the tab on his zipper down a few teeth, her knuckle grazing the sensitive skin of his pelvis. His stomach muscles contracted. "I'm no Mother Teresa."

"Really? Tell me how you'd like to suck my cock without using anatomically correct language," he challenged her. She could hear amusement, as well as an underlying curiosity. As long as she didn't back down he wasn't going to either. He was pushing to see how far she'd go.

She'd already gone pretty far. A little farther wouldn't hurt her.

"I want to suck your—" She rolled the word around on her tongue but couldn't make it come out of her mouth. Talking straight up dirty was going to take her more time. "I'd rather show you," she said. She eased the zipper on his jeans all the way down, then slid her palms into the open flap. Inside his jockey briefs he was already hard. She went to her knees.

"Wait." His voice was thick. He lifted her to her feet. "Not here."

If they were going to do this, then this time, he was doing things right. She wasn't giving him a blowjob in front of a window with the curtains drawn back that had a camera aimed at it.

And as hot as he found it to hear Dr. Babe say things that would make a men's rugby team blush, sex didn't always have to be down and dirty. He liked hearing her cry out his name. He wouldn't mind finding out how it sounded coming on a soft, panting moan either.

She didn't ask questions as to why the change of heart—and location—which was a relief, although in the back of his head he did have to wonder why, when it was so obvious she knew he was lying to her, she didn't call him on it. That was a puzzle he'd have to figure out later—the same as he'd have to decide how he'd play this with Dan. Lying to his team leader was all kinds of wrong.

He backed Irina into the hall leading to the bedrooms at the back of the house. As soon as they rounded the corner he had her against the wall. He linked his fingers with hers and stretched her arms over her head. He thrust one knee between her thighs. He'd been thinking about this all week. How he'd like to touch her. How he'd like to take her. He'd fantasized the details each time she'd bent over to retrieve her bowling ball from the return in those tight yoga pants tonight too. He'd been dying to discover why those panty lines were missing. Dear God, please let it be a thong. He loved thongs.

Maybe down and dirty wasn't off the table just yet after all.

He dropped his mouth to her throat, slowly licking the tip of his tongue to her ear. She tasted as good as he remembered—a little salt and all kinds of sweet. He took the lobe in his teeth, then sucked on it. She caught her breath, arching her body, her crotch on his knee, her breasts pressing against his pounding ribs. His jeans were hanging off his hips, his erection straining the front of his briefs.

"I want to fuck you right here," he panted.

Definitely not off the table.

He fought for control. What the hell was wrong with him that he couldn't wait the time it took to walk twenty more paces to get to a bed?

Irina ground against his thigh. "I'm not stopping you."

She turned her head so her lips were on his. She thrust her tongue into his mouth.

He let go of her hands to seize the top of her stretchy pants. Just as he'd suspected, his fingers caught on the lacy strings of a thong, trailing it to the single thread that disappeared between two round, firm cheeks. He let out a groan, half tortured, half disappointed. He was going to be so sorry he'd missed seeing this later. Right now, he wanted it gone. He tugged her pants and her panties as far as her knees. He freed his erection from his briefs. He grabbed both of those cheeks in his hands and lifted her higher, cradling her in position against the wall, and with a hard thrust and bend of his knees, slid deep inside her.

She had her arms around his neck, holding him tight. He rested his forehead against hers, trying to regain self-control. He was banging her against a wall. This should be good for them both, not just him.

"Tell me how you like it," he said. "What you want me to do to you. Where you want me to do it." If she said she wanted a bed it was going to kill him.

"Here. Right now. I like it this way, slow and deep. I like having you inside me." He could feel each shallow breath she couldn't quite catch. Each little quiver of excitement as her tight inner muscles began squeezing around him. Quiet, pretty, brainy little Dr. Babe was closer to coming than he was.

And that was *so* freaking hot.

He drove his hips upward, forcing himself deeper inside her, taking it as slow as he could. He lifted her slightly, then lowered her again, repeating the pattern over and over. Her fists curled in his hair. His arms started shaking, but from the coming orgasm, not the minimal effort it took to support her slight frame. She hooked her heels around the backs of his thighs. Somehow, she'd managed to get free of her pants. He buried his face against the side of her throat, nipping and sucking the skin, feeling her whole body tense as she came.

"Oh, my God," she cried out.

His own orgasm rocked him to the soles of his feet.

That, he thought dimly as he leaned one shoulder against the wall for support, holding her with him still inside her, had been well worth the wait. He'd had an entire week of frustration. He'd have plenty of time for remorse later. Right now, he had much better plans that involved getting his hands—and his mouth—on the two soft breasts still contained by a bra beneath her shirt.

He hiked her hips higher so her legs were wrapped around his waist. Her arms clutched his neck, her head limp on his shoulder, her face pressed into the collar of his half-undone shirt. Her cheek was damp with a fine layer of perspiration that had him semi-hard with satisfaction. He'd done that to her.

He stepped out of the jeans puddled around his ankles and kicked them aside. They'd gotten down and dirty out of the way. He had plenty more moves to show her. They were just getting started. "Your bed or mine?"

"Yours."

She said it without hesitation, confirming his suspicion that she didn't want him in her bedroom. There was no point in being insulted by it. He had a world he didn't want her to be part of. She was entitled to keep him out of hers. The difference was that he wanted to keep her out for her own good. He came in contact with the sleaziest of people. Extreme Sports Guy was the tip of the iceberg. A few pop-ups and botnets were nothing compared to the things he'd seen.

That made his reasons better than hers.

Maybe he couldn't help being a little insulted after all.

Hours later, when they were both too tired to move but neither was ready to fall asleep, Kale rolled to his stomach and draped an arm around Irina's waist so she couldn't ease out of bed and escape as he suspected she'd like.

She was pretty open to experimentation. He'd pushed her, but he'd been very careful to make sure she could say no any time she liked. She hadn't, even though he'd had to talk her through a few things because she hadn't been familiar with the mechanics involved. He wasn't sure what her willingness indicated—whether she thought he was just all that—or if she figured after a few weeks she'd never see him again and could pretend nothing outside of her normal comfort zone had taken place. What happened in Vegas…

They'd see about that.

"How do you feel about bondage?" he asked.

She looked at him, all wide, wary eyes and tangled hair on the pillow they shared. "You don't need to tie me up. I don't think I could move if I tried."

He had to smile. "I didn't mean this very second. I was asking for future reference. You know. For next time."

A sudden stillness spread through her. "Is there going to be a next time?"

"Well, sure," he said. "Why stop now?" She'd initiated this evening. She'd been on board with everything they'd done. And it had been outstanding. Hadn't it? "Don't tell me you've lost interest already."

"Last time you were the one who had second thoughts."

He propped his head on his hand so he could see her more clearly. The room was warm despite the slight breeze from the open window above the bed. Shadows spilled into the corners, but there was enough light for him to be able to read her expression. Any second now she was going to launch into a discussion about boundaries between them that he did not want to have. Not until he found out how far those boundaries could be stretched to his advantage.

"Let's get something clear," he said. "I did not, in any way, shape or form, have second thoughts. The situation got complicated. That's all."

"Is it any less complicated now?"

She had him there. "No. But I didn't know bondage might be part of the deal. So…is it?"

"I'm not saying no. We can talk about it." Her cheeks dimpled. "It depends on how *you* feel about toys?"

He'd love to ask her to name a sex toy. He didn't believe she could do it. He did, however, believe she was willing to try them. And that fried a few more of his brain cells where she was concerned. "Babe. Please don't mess with me. You're raising expectations I'm not sure I can fulfill. At least not tonight."

She wriggled under the weight of his arm, trying to lift it off her. "Then I should be going."

He tightened his hold. He didn't want her to leave. He liked having her here, in his bed. It was a double and he took up most of the space, which meant full-body contact was unavoidable.

"Stay. Talk to me for a bit." With any luck she'd fall asleep, although he'd been pretty lucky already tonight. "Tell me more about your family," he coaxed her. "What was it like growing up with a Russian father and a Canadian mother?"

And with that, the mood of the evening was broken. Dr. Glasov emerged, tetchy and defensive.

"If you're wondering if there's a link between my father and the RBN, there isn't. He always swore he came to Canada to be a Canadian. My mother wasn't allowed to keep any Russian traditions for him. He speaks English as if he were born here. And since my mother's illness he's been focused on her one hundred percent. He doesn't have time for espionage."

"That wasn't where I was going with the question," Kale said, "but it's useful information all the same, so thanks." He cupped her cheek in his palm, running his thumb over her lips. "You don't often engage in pillow talk, do you?"

She had her hand on his hip, idly drawing circles with the tip of her finger. "I had no idea there were rules. Since you're the expert, why don't you show me how it's done? What was it like growing up in so many different countries?"

"I was always the new kid. I had my ass handed to me all over the Middle East before I learned how to take care of myself. That wore thin pretty quick too, so I learned how to make friends instead. After that it was fun."

"I find it hard to believe there were that many boys willing to take on someone your size."

"I wasn't always this size." And there was a distinct advantage in numbers. She didn't need to know about that.

"What about your family? What are they like?"

"Besides my parents, I have three brothers. I'm the oldest by eight years. There's a rumor I might have arrived seven or eight months shy of their first anniversary, but they aren't sharing the wedding date so it remains unconfirmed. My youngest brother's fifteen. He's showing a lot of promise as a soccer player. The other two are in university. One's in the UK, the other is in the United States. My dad's still a diplomat. I think he's in Greece right now. My mom keeps him tolerable. She follows him wherever he goes and loves being his social coordinator. My grandparents on his side live in a retirement village near Ottawa. They don't travel much anymore. My mother's mother lives in Fredericton. She's a going concern, but refuses to leave New Brunswick."

"Fredericton's only a four hour drive from here. Have you been to visit your grandmother?"

She had no idea he was in Canada right now, so his visit wouldn't be missed. He'd been meaning to make the time, but then he'd been asked to follow Irina.

"Would you like to go with me?" he heard himself ask, shocking the hell out of him.

She took her time answering, as usual. "I know we're pretending to be a couple in public. But shouldn't we try and keep things as professional as possible between us in our personal lives?"

Disappointment cut through his shock. He hadn't expected her to say yes. They weren't forming any long-term relationship. They both knew that was impossible. Keeping things professional, however? After tonight?

That was too far a stretch.

"I can see your point," he said. "You'd meet my grandmother, then I'd have to meet your parents to level the playing field, and before you know it we're sleeping together. We wouldn't want that to happen."

"God forbid." She snuggled against him, all smooth, naked skin and soft, kissable curves, sliding her knee between his thighs and tucking her head under his chin. She curled her arms between them so that both palms rested on his chest, then yawned. "I promise I won't make a habit of sleeping in here, but I'm literally too tired to crawl out of bed."

He had no problem with that. She was right where he wanted her. He drew the cotton sheet up around them and kissed the top of her head. Once he got into her bed—and he would—he'd use the same excuse to spend the night there.

"OK. But this means you're cooking breakfast," he said.

CHAPTER TEN

SUNLIGHT POURED ACROSS THE bed in the spare room. The shower was running in the guest bathroom, but it was Kale's cell phone vibrating on the bedside table that had awoken Irina. Someone was sending him a text message at 6:58 in the morning.

Her brain fully reengaged and heat scalded her body. Last night he hadn't had to talk her into anything. She'd volunteered to do it all on her own. And she'd proved she was no Mother Teresa.

The cell phone fell silent. She heard the shower shut off and scrambled out of bed. That was her cue to leave. The last time she'd woken up without any clothes on she'd had to pretend to be comfortable walking around naked, but in reality, it was a whole lot easier to be cool and collected when fully dressed. She didn't want him thinking she expected more from him than sex. She wasn't going to be that woman—the one who didn't know how to walk away when the fun times were over. She'd already used the lamest excuse possible to spend the whole night with him. Again. Where was her pride?

By the time he emerged from the bathroom, she was in front of the open fridge door in the kitchen wearing a bathrobe and slippers. He had on a pair of navy board shorts and, she suspected from the way they hung off his hips, nothing else. His skin was damp from the shower. He'd tied his wet hair in the usual knot. The way those blue eyes examined her, as if he were recalling in vivid detail every intimate thing that they'd done, sucked all the air from her lungs and had her heart attempting a jail break.

She'd never had sex on her kitchen counter. Broad daylight, however, made it much more difficult to suggest. There was a lot to be said for the cover of darkness.

"We're having an omelet and fresh fruit for breakfast," she announced. "Lunch will be soup and a salad. We can't keep eating pizza."

She caught a glimpse of those white teeth as he folded his arms across his bare chest and leaned against the island to watch her work. "If you're trying to starve me, do your worst. I've gone for three days without eating real food before. I'll survive your fresh fruit and salad." He tugged at a lock of her hair. His tone changed, becoming more serious. "I've got a work-related thing to do in the city this morning. What's on your agenda? Can I drop you off somewhere? Any friends you want to hang out with for a few hours? What about Bev?" He grinned. "She seems like fun."

That must have been what the text was about. She appreciated his consideration for not wanting to leave her alone when he knew it still made her nervous, but he had a job to do and not everything about it involved her. Besides, sometimes it was difficult for her to work when he was around and he was a definite distraction today. Last night should have taken the edge off, but no. A few hours apart might be good for them both.

"Why don't you drop me at my office?" she suggested.

"I can work on the computer there until I get my laptop cleaned up."

Humor licked at his lips. "Have you ever considered doing something more…recreational on a Saturday?"

The counter again came to mind. She took the carton of eggs from the fridge and got a glass mixing bowl from the cupboard under the island. "You're working today too."

"Not the whole day." He reached for the cutting board and a knife, and picked up the cantaloupe she'd already set out. "I can survive your healthy breakfast, but how about we skip the soup and salad and I take you somewhere for a late lunch with more substance?"

She was so, so tempted. But she'd never embarked on a strictly sexual relationship before and didn't know how these things worked. They were currently sharing a residence, complicating things further. Having him take her out for lunch, especially after last night, sounded too much like something real couples might do. This wasn't her simply tagging along while he went surfing or climbing. Common sense whispered, *Say no*.

Kale's gaze, locked on her face, never wavered. "You're thinking too much again, Dr. Babe. I'll make it easier for you. Here's how things will be. I'm going to leave you at your office until twelve or twelve thirty. After that, we're taking a drive to the Annapolis Valley. There's a winery in Grand Pré with a restaurant attached to it that I'd like to check out. We'll do a little sightseeing too. And in the meantime, if you want to think about anything other than work, you can think about tonight. I know that's what's going to be on my mind all day." His eyes filled with a heat that made her toes curl inside her slippers. "Unfortunately, before any of that can happen, I have a meeting to get to."

Against her better judgment, she heard herself agreeing. After all, what could it hurt?

"You might not want to open any emails from yourself," Kale advised her as he stopped the car at the door of her office building.

He was kidding, but she'd already thought of that. She did send emails to herself at the office. She also notified the admin assistant if she was working out of the office and kept the department director apprised of her progress on any project deliverables. She sometimes had a junior staff member do research for her. Everyone got emails from her.

This was why cyber intrusions were so difficult to contain.

Kale waited until she was inside. She waved from the foyer, watching as he drove away. She then signed in with the commissionaire on duty and took the elevator to her floor.

The offices in her department were empty, which wasn't unusual considering it was a Saturday. This morning, however, felt different, as if someone were staring over her shoulder, which was ridiculous. She'd worked after hours on plenty of occasions. No one could get in or out of the building without a security pass. The commissionaires patrolled the floors on a staggered schedule to avoid predictability.

The problem was that she didn't have Kale here to make her feel safe and that was a problem she'd have to overcome. He wasn't her bodyguard. He collected intelligence, and pop-ups and botnets simply weren't worth his time. Only her professional reputation had kept CSIS interested this far. She suspected the same could be said about Kale's personal interest in her. He liked getting dirty with prim and proper Dr. Glasov. She was a challenge he couldn't resist. Eventually, though, the novelty would wear off. When it did, and CSIS's interest in her situation was satisfied, he'd be gone.

She didn't want to think about that.

Once she was inside her office with the door locked behind her she felt more at ease. She started her desktop computer and ran the antivirus program just to be safe. It appeared to be clean. Nothing lurked in her spam folder. She plugged in her thumb drive and ran a check on it too. So far so good.

She was engrossed in revising the paper she was presenting in Paris next month when the pop-up appeared, catching her completely off guard. It was a video, dark and grainy, and of such poor quality that it took a second for her preoccupied brain to process the images she was seeing. When it did there was no mistake. Although her face was a blur, it was definitely her. She was doing a striptease in front of her living room window with Kale on the sofa in the background behind her. His face, too, was obscured, but she knew every inch of those muscular legs. She had her thumbs under her bra straps, sliding first one, then the other, off her shoulders. The rest of the events unfolded much faster than she remembered, but it was all there—right down to her straddling Kale's thighs with an enthusiasm that photographed well.

Blood rushed to her head, pounding so hard in her ears that her vision went black. She grabbed the edge of her desk with both hands, afraid of passing out. That pop-up had come in through the company's intranet. She had no idea how far it might have already spread. Thank God the department was empty. If this had been Monday morning, there would be no hope of stopping it.

Forget about company rules regarding security and how to deal with Internet threats. She had to contain this.

By the time she finished, Irina was confused about some things but clearer on others. She cupped her forehead in her hands, her elbows on her desk, thinking it through. The pop-up was fairly basic and easily removed. It had come in through her intranet connection, the same as the others, and been targeted specifically at her. She could find no signs of it anywhere else. The big question remained—who would do such a thing? And why?

If the video had come from inside the department, then whoever had done this had to know there was nothing to gain by phishing. Classified information simply wouldn't show up on non-dedicated computers. She had no access to it when she was working alone. She had to sign for the key to the room and it required one other signature, usually the production manager's or that of the administrative assistant. That meant her after-hours work at the office mainly involved correspondence and research.

From the corner of her eye she caught sight of the time. It was 1:07. A quick check of the parking lot through her window showed that Kale was waiting for her, patient as always. She had no idea how long he'd been there. He had his feet on the dash and no doubt the radio cranked up full blast.

She backed up her files and ejected her thumb drive from her computer, then gathered her things. As she waited for the elevator the numbness and shock began to wear off. Logic returned. Someone was harassing her. Spying on her home. Invading her privacy. While she'd known that already the steadiness and angle of the image suggested the camera was mounted. She hadn't suspected for a moment there might be a surveillance camera trained on her front window 24/7. She tried to imagine how Kale would react when she told him about it.

She went cold all over. How *would* he react?

Her light-headedness returned as she followed the train of events. The night the video was taken they'd had sex in her living room. He'd encouraged her not to be so uptight. He'd seemed fine when they woke up the next morning, if somewhat insultingly anxious to curtail any expectations on her part. It wasn't until after he'd taken a walk around her property that things had become truly strained between them. She'd chalked it up to him being indiscreet and telling his boss about them, but now, she had to ask herself—what had precipitated that call to his handler in the first place? Why had he been told that sex with her was off limits? Why, last night, had he not wanted to have sex in the living room, but was OK with it up against the wall in the hallway?

Because he'd discovered that camera. That was the only logical conclusion.

She was seriously afraid she'd throw up. She might have gotten rid of the pop-up, but the video with the original content remained at large in the world.

The elevator arrived. The doors slid apart, loud in the empty reception area, and she stepped inside on unsteady legs. She wanted so much to give Kale the benefit of the doubt, but if he'd even suspected the possibility of a video and said nothing to warn her he'd better have a good explanation.

A message from Dan asking for a meeting wasn't the way Kale had planned to kick start his morning. They'd arranged a rendezvous in the parking lot of a local sportsplex where it wouldn't seem strange for two men to sit in a car and carry on a conversation.

As he waited for Dan to arrive Kale's thoughts refused to shift far from Irina. She was Dr. Jekyll and a really hot Mrs. Hyde—minus the murderous inclinations. He'd never been so turned on by a fuzzy pink bathrobe and matching slippers in his life, probably because he knew that underneath it her preference in underwear was lacy pink thongs. Pink was his new favorite color. He couldn't seem to get enough of it. Or of her.

Dan had asked for this meeting. If this was about his personal relationship with Irina he planned to tell Dan that what they did together in private was none of his business. Kale was here unofficially and she wasn't under investigation so there was no conflict of interest. He'd give up his vacation time if he had to. The trade-off would be worth it.

The passenger door of his car creaked open and his team leader hopped in. At thirty-seven Dan Hanson was the epitome of average, at least in physical appearance. Underneath the tax-auditor exterior he had the nerves of a cliff diver. A former intelligence officer with a background in psychology and anti-terrorism, he'd given up fieldwork two years ago to sit behind a desk.

Kale's work too was normally focused on anti-terrorism, which was how he'd found himself on Dan's team. Meeting Irina had been dumb luck, a simple case of being in the right place at the right time.

"Public transportation in this city leaves a lot to be desired," Dan complained. "I gave up and rented a car at the airport."

Enough with the small talk. If there was going to be bad news Kale wanted it straight up. "What's so important that you had to tell me in person?"

"And hello to you too," Dan replied. Amusement flashed for an instant in eyes that normally lacked any tells. The team leader kept his cards close to his chest. "Dr. Glasov's connection to the RBN could be part of a larger problem. I told you before that the director is trying to keep a lid on certain information. We currently have a Canadian citizen under investigation. He's an old friend of the Minister of National Defence. He operates abroad using the RBN as part of his network for transporting stolen military weapons systems parts. He has a clever system for private communication with his daughter over the Internet too. The intelligence officer assigned to that case is here in Nova Scotia, visiting family. I'm trying to decide if I should turn Dr. Glasov and her cyber issues over to him. If I do that it means opening a new case file and I'd be shining a light on her at a higher level. The lid would be off."

The friendship with an expat of questionable morals explained why the director didn't want sensitive information going to the defense minister's office right now. There was likely a whole lot more to that story too. But all Kale really heard was Dan suggesting someone else might be handed responsibility for Irina.

That wasn't going to happen. "There's no need to open a case file on her. I'm OK with staying right where I am."

"I'm sure you are." Dan's cool gaze said he saw right through Kale and his motives. "However. The RBN is already a common denominator. Considering the nature of Dr. Glasov's work I'd really like to know if there's any connection between her pop-ups and botnets and those missing military parts—or if a Canadian expat named Marc Leon Beausejour factors in anywhere."

"The name doesn't ring any bells," Kale said slowly. "But if you're looking for connections, why not investigate Irina's father? She says he was a sort of journalist translator in the former Soviet Union. Maybe someone's trying to get to him through her. Maybe he hasn't entirely forgotten the motherland. Or been forgotten by it either."

Dan drummed his fingers on his knee and stared out the windshield, a frown of concentration on his face. "Anton Glasov isn't a problem," he finally admitted. "He was working for the Canadian government in Russia. That's why he defected here. If Dr. Glasov goes back a generation or two she'll find she has less Russian in her family tree than he's led her to believe. Once he met and married her mother he dropped out of the spy game completely. His choice. And while it's possible someone might be using his daughter to try and get to him I can't see why. The wall is down. He hasn't been active anywhere in more than thirty years. No, Dr. Glasov's work is a far more likely target than he is."

And they'd established that her work was only accessible through her head. Kale's gut clenched. He handed Dan the file folder he'd grabbed from the backseat of the car. "Here's the printed list of Irina's email contacts. I didn't see the name Beausejour anywhere on it."

Dan examined the folder. "Did you get a list of contacts from her workplace computer too?"

"No," Kale admitted. He'd gotten...sidetracked. "I'll ask her for one."

"If you can get it to me before my flight leaves tonight, I'd appreciate it." Dan scanned the names. "Baby Jesus. Between them these people could take over the world. Or destroy it."

"Now you see why I didn't want to email the list to you."

"I keep expecting this piece of paper to catch fire and self-destruct." Dan hummed the theme music from *Mission Impossible* as he tucked it back in the folder. He tapped the edge of the folder against his thigh. "My other reason for coming here was to tell you that you're needed in London, but now I have to figure out what to do about Dr. Glasov."

Kale feigned an indifference he didn't feel, reluctant to reveal how much his team leader's decision mattered to him. This definitely wasn't the time to tell Dan to mind his own damn business about Kale's relationship with Irina.

A group of adolescent boys carrying matching kit bags with team logos passed in front of the car, laughing and pushing each other as they headed for the entrance to the pool.

"I've already established a cover," he said, watching as the boys shoved their way through the doors, each jockeying for first place. "Someone new would have to come in and start over fresh. Why not send another intelligence officer to London?"

"I don't have anyone else who knows both Farsi and Arabic." Dan's careful expression said he had more to say. Kale waited for it. "I could buy you two weeks. In return you'd have to convince Dr. Glasov to hack into the RBN for CSIS and tell us what's going on."

"If you're trying to bribe me you should know that what you're offering isn't a carrot. It's a stick."

"Don't bullshit me, Martin. I'm not stupid. We both know you're still sleeping with her. If you weren't you'd have your bags packed and be halfway to London by now. Two weeks," he repeated. "Take it or leave it."

He was going to take it, but it wasn't nearly enough time. "Why not have CSEC do the dirty work for you?"

"Because we don't want the minister's office to find out what's going on," Dan reminded him. "We also don't want to leave a trail leading back to the Canadian government." He handed Kale a thumb drive. "This is a ghost VPN. I'm assured it's so secure that Dr. Glasov can be in and out of any network, no matter where it is, and no one will ever know she was there. Even if she's caught, under the circumstances no one would question her motives for hacking into the RBN. The Russians might question ours though, since the FSB uses the RBN for some of its cyber operations."

More and more, Kale didn't like what he was hearing. The FSB was the Federal Security Service of the Russian Federation—the Russian equivalent of the American Federal Bureau of Investigation.

"Say she's in, she's not caught, but she finds nothing. What happens to her after the two weeks are up? What if there aren't any new leads?" Who would protect her?

Dan's gaze narrowed. "We aren't a babysitting service. She's being harassed, yes, but so far everything's been personal and that's not our problem. Other than her email list getting spammed there's no real proof anyone's after her designs. She hasn't been physically threatened either. We'll tap her phone and monitor her travel. The RCMP will be directed to have someone keep an eye on her house for a few months in case things escalate. That's the best we can do."

Kale had never been one of those guys who could turn

the safety of the people he cared about over to others. And he did care about Irina. Not only was two weeks not long enough to find out who was cyberstalking her and why, he had a sneaking suspicion he wouldn't have grown tired of her by the end of them. He doubted if she'd be done with him either. Not if last night was any indicator. But he had no real choice in the matter. His main work was anti-terrorism not espionage. Two weeks was all he had.

This was why he tried to keep his relationships casual. Good-byes could be messy and he hated being the bad guy.

He slid the thumb drive into his pocket. "I'll see what I can do but she was pretty adamant about not wanting to have anything to do with the RBN. She's a weapons systems placement designer not an Internet security expert. She sure as hell isn't a spy."

Dan opened the car door and got out. He leaned his head in. "I have faith in you. After all, you talked her into bed. Try using some more of that charm. If you can't keep it zipped you might as well put it to good use."

"You're a dick," Kale said.

Dan laughed. He patted the roof of the car. "I'll see you in London in two weeks."

Traffic was light on the highway as Kale drove back to the airport to pick up Irina. When he arrived there were only two other cars in the parking lot.

He glanced at the dashboard clock. He was a few minutes late. She wasn't at the door waiting for him, meaning she'd gotten immersed in her work, and he had no idea when she might resurface. He rolled the windows down, cranked up the radio, and reclined his seat, getting comfortable. It could be worse. At least she wasn't a shopper. Keeping tabs on her in a crowd would be a nightmare.

At 1:17 she emerged.

Rather than get out of the car to help carry her laptop as he normally would he stayed where he was and watched her approach. God, she was pretty. He couldn't decide if it was good luck that he'd been assigned to her or a personal disaster. Two weeks were nothing.

She'd tucked loose waves of her long, light brown hair behind her ears. A casual breeze tossed the tendrils so that she had to capture her hair with her free hand to keep it from tangling in knots. Over a pair of pale gray, conservative shorts she wore a cropped, darker gray sweatshirt, perfectly acceptable weekend office attire. A stack of silver bangles jangled from the slender wrist of the hand gripping her laptop.

It was hard to get his head around a woman who looked like a timid pixie possessing the kind of intelligence she did. It was harder still to imagine her panting his name while he was deep inside her, his pants around his ankles and her back pressed to a wall, and yet that had happened. He hated the possibility of any harm coming to her. He didn't want to think about the two week time frame he was working with either.

The thumb drive burned a hole in his pocket. His gut and his conscience told him it was wrong to ask her to hack into the RBN. She was a scientist not a spy. She knew full well what the risks of such an action were, probably better than he did. If CSIS was going to "shine a light on her," as Dan had put it, then Kale would far rather that light come from the Minister of Defence's office than Russian organized crime. In her line of work the FSB would be equally bad. Either way her professional reputation could take a serious beating.

She put her laptop in the backseat before joining him in the front of the car. He took one look at those long-lashed green eyes as she fished for the seat belt and his stomach constricted. Something had happened. Her whole body language was too stiff.

So much for his good luck. This day had been headed straight to hell from the get-go.

"What's wrong?" he asked.

"Another pop-up on my work computer." She latched the seat belt with a loud click. Her fingers were shaking and she refused to meet his gaze. "I managed to get rid of it, at least for now. I don't think it spread. I have no idea if it will come back though."

Her voice was quiet. Controlled and remote. Very much Dr. Glasov and he didn't like it. It meant she was furious and the most likely target was him. The constriction in his stomach spread to his lungs. His heart pummeled his ribs. If she'd gone to the trouble of removing a pop-up after explaining to him that the company she was working for had their own IT security protocol for such things, then he had a good idea what it contained.

"I can explain," he said.

"I doubt it. But you're welcome to give it a shot."

While he didn't blame her for being angry he wasn't getting into a fight with her in the parking lot of her workplace. There were security cameras everywhere and she had a professional reputation to protect. He preferred to take this somewhere she couldn't walk away from him either, but that would still be discreet. He couldn't imagine Irina—and especially not Dr. Glasov—making a public scene.

He brought his seat upright and turned the key in the ignition. "We'll talk over lunch."

CHAPTER ELEVEN

THE FIFTY MINUTE DRIVE to the Annapolis Valley region of the province was nerve-wracking, at least from Kale's perspective.

Irina was silent which meant she was thinking. No good ever came of that. It would help if he knew how bad that video was, but he wasn't about to incriminate himself further by asking the wrong questions. There was the possibility that he might be wrong—that the pop-up wasn't of them in her living room at a really bad time and in a few eyebrow-raising positions. He'd let her do the talking so he could get a sense of how best to proceed.

But so far she wasn't talking.

He took Exit 10 off the highway onto a main road that meandered through quaint towns and field after rolling field of apple trees and grape vines. After another ten minutes of silence he turned into the drive of the winery he'd chosen for a late lunch. Acres of vineyard stretched uphill toward the base of the North Mountain, which formed a natural barricade against the high tides of the Bay of Fundy on the far side.

The mid-August heat body-slammed them as they got out of the air-conditioned car. The air was humid and heavy, filled with the smells of irrigated earth and the flowers scattered in beds around the winery buildings and paths. They walked a shrouded, rock-walled lane to the restaurant positioned behind the outlet wine store.

It was shortly after two o'clock and the main part of the restaurant was empty. The hostess led them to a cozy table near a rustic stone hearth. While they looked at the menus Kale ordered a coffee for him and tea for Irina. Once they were alone he broke the silence. She'd had more than enough time to think. He wanted to know what was going on inside her head.

"If I've done something wrong, then tell me straight up. The silent treatment is a little junior high, don't you think?"

She looked up from her menu, blinking those lovely green eyes. "I wouldn't know."

Because she'd skipped junior high. She could be so deadpan sometimes. He fought back a smile of relief. She didn't sound as if she were still angry but it was difficult to tell. She didn't always react the way he'd expect.

"Why don't you tell me about the new pop-up?" he prompted her.

"Why don't you tell me why you didn't see fit to mention the surveillance camera aimed at my living room window?" she countered. "I'm going to give you the benefit of the doubt and assume you didn't know about it before we had sex on my sofa with the curtains wide open."

There went any hope he'd harbored, slight as it was, that he'd been mistaken about the pop-up's subject matter. She was most definitely still angry about it too. At least she hadn't mentioned that he'd been the one to encourage her to leave those curtains drawn back. That was a positive sign.

"I didn't know. I swear. Once I found the camera I reported it. We decided to leave it in place so whoever put it there wouldn't be scared off. We hoped they might come back for it. So far they haven't." He played with his knife, weighing the risks of trying to lighten the mood. What the hell. He might as well go all in. "Out of curiosity. Did the video make me look fat?"

She cast him a look only diminished in its death ray effect by a stream of sunlight that captured the light dusting of freckles across the bridge of her nose. "And to think I'm the one being too junior high."

Oh yeah. She was mad.

"Look on the bright side. That computer degree came in handy. You got rid of the pop-up before anyone else saw it," he said.

"The degree works best when you're causing the chaos, not doing damage control. I only got rid of one instance of it. Once things go online they're out there forever. Don't forget someone still has the original too." She crumpled her cloth napkin between her fingers, then smoothed it out flat. "The quality is poor and our faces aren't clear. While our mothers might recognize us it would never stand up in court. That's the one positive in all this."

He should have known she'd be practical once she got over the shock. Letting her have that time in the car to think had been the right thing to do after all. "I guess that explains why I'm still alive."

"This isn't funny."

"No it isn't," he admitted.

He sat back in his chair. He'd gotten his personal and professional lives intertwined and while he felt guilty as hell about digging her deeper into a situation already disturbing to her, he had a problem now too. Thanks to her fancy degrees and an impressive list of peers her professional reputation would likely survive a poor quality sex tape. His employer might not be as willing to overlook it and being forced to take a desk job would kill him. He was a field agent.

"You aren't alone in that video, Irina. This might come as a surprise, all things considered, but I'm not into exhibitionism. Or voyeurism for that matter. What goes on between two consenting adults is nobody else's business. I don't need the whole world sizing my junk or judging my performance. And yeah. This impacts my career so I'm angry too." He might not be an exhibitionist or into voyeurism, but he seized opportunities when they arose. If he was ever going to get her to hack into the RBN this was his chance. He had to push the right buttons. "I want them stopped as badly as you do."

The waitress returned with their coffee and tea. They placed their meal orders and she gathered the menus before once again leaving them alone.

Irina lifted the small silver pot the waitress had left beside her napkin and poured a stream of steaming orange pekoe into a white porcelain cup. A frown marred her brow. "We don't know what whoever's behind this is after. We don't know who they are. Why hasn't CSIS used their resources to go online after them by now?"

"About that," Kale began, uneasy again. She still believed he was here in an official capacity. He was and he wasn't. He didn't know if she'd fully appreciate the subtleties of that distinction. "I met with my team leader this morning. He claims CSIS doesn't want anyone on the other side of the RBN to track their activity back to the Canadian government. The Russian government is known to use the RBN too. It could be viewed as an act of hostility."

"Posting porn videos of unsuspecting participants isn't hostile? Doesn't the fact that the RBN is being used to harass a Canadian citizen mean anything? Especially one who does the work I do?" Her frown deepened into suspicion. "CSIS could have been monitoring activity from this end, but it's obvious they're not. What's going on? What aren't you telling me?"

He dodged the question. "CSIS wants you to hack into the RBN for them. You have the right security clearances already in place."

She laughed without mirth. "I get the importance of international relations. I understand why they don't want to do it themselves. The difference, however, is that the person doing the hacking at CSIS would be faceless. I'm not. It's my life and reputation on the line."

"You're being dramatic." Guilt pinched his conscience as he pushed another button. She was the least dramatic person he knew.

Her gaze sharpened. "I disagree."

She was trying to decide what game he was playing. Or more likely what team he was on. He withdrew the thumb drive from his pocket and set it on the table between them. "You'd be anonymous. They gave you a ghost VPN."

She didn't pick it up. Hurt filled her eyes as she figured out he was Team CSIS, and his gut wrenched. He had no choice. He wasn't so much Team CSIS as Team Doing-What's-Right.

"One they could use themselves," she said, quick to recover. "Or anyone could use. I find it hard to believe a spy agency doesn't have better-trained cyber security resources than me. So why ask me to do it? What do they hope to accomplish?" She folded her arms on the table and leaned toward him. "It isn't anything that will benefit me. If they were truly interested in my welfare we wouldn't be having this discussion."

While he didn't like spilling government secrets Kale was going to have to be more upfront with her. She was being asked to do what amounted as a favor to CSIS on faith. She was too smart to accept one-sided terms without a reasonable explanation, and yet he couldn't tell her about the possible connection between the RBN and another, higher priority case.

He returned the thumb drive to his pocket. "There's been a security breach at CSIS. Any new cases are being vetted by the department's director before information can be passed on. We can't ask CSEC—the Communications Security Establishment of Canada—to assist, which is what we'd normally do. They're the ones with the cyber security talent. And that right there is more than I'm authorized to tell you," he said lightly. "Don't make me have to kill you."

She didn't respond to his feeble attempt at a joke. Of course not. She'd never be deflected by humor. She'd be focused more on the information he gave her and sifting out what was important. He waited for the explosion when she drew her conclusions.

Their lunches arrived. He dug into pan fried halibut and roasted red potatoes. Irina's garden salad remained untouched in front of her.

She settled her napkin on her lap. "CSIS doesn't believe I have a real problem," she said. "This whole time the only action they've taken, based on what I've told you, has been to get you to go bowling with me."

He took as long as he could to chew a mouthful of food, choosing his next words with caution. "I'm here aren't I? They know who you are. Until this security breach at the agency is sorted out though, pop-ups and botnets that don't have access to sensitive documents simply aren't high priorities for them."

"Then why *are* you still here? To convince me to do CSIS's work for them? What if I won't do it? How much longer will you stick around if I say no?"

He set his fork on the edge of his plate. The conversation kept teetering on the edge of professional and personal, something he wasn't used to. This was another good reason to keep those two areas separate in his life from now on. Lesson learned—although far too late in this particular instance. He didn't know how she felt, but for his part he had no wish to extricate himself from their personal relationship yet. She had layers that he liked exploring. She was smart. Too smart for him really. She made him think. And while hardly a risk taker she was pretty and sweet, adventurous and fun in her own quiet way.

"Whether you agree to do it or not I'm here for two more weeks," he said.

"I see."

With those two quiet, accusatory words the conversation teetered over to personal. Somewhere, in another part of the restaurant, a door opened and closed. Other than that small sign of life they were temporarily alone.

"I don't think you do." He wasn't having her think she was nothing but casual sex to him. That ship had sailed the first time she'd used the term *labia minora* to talk dirty. "I don't give a damn if you do what CSIS wants. I'm here for you and I'm staying as long as I can. But at the end of the day I've got a job to do too. One I feel pretty strongly about. I have another assignment that begins in two weeks and it's out of the country. I'm not sure when I'll be able to see you again after that."

Her gaze remained cool. "I'm not asking you to make some sort of commitment to me. We'd agreed this was a temporary arrangement. The only thing difficult about it is living under the same roof. It makes things...complicated." She lifted her slender shoulders. The bangles on her wrist tinkled together as she picked at her salad. "It doesn't matter if CSIS doesn't believe my problem is real. I know it is, and since you're the only person I trust, in two weeks I'm back on my own."

The memory of the look in her eyes when he'd first come to her door and sat in her kitchen flooded back to him. She was scared and there was very little he could do about it. His fingers tightened. He felt the same as he had that day on the beach when the investment broker with the sketchy friends had approached her—protective and territorial. And while the fact that her bedroom remained off-limits made it quite clear how she thought things between them should be, no matter how Dr. Babe wished to play things he didn't believe for a second that he was any more casual to her than she was to him.

He had a responsibility here. If he wanted to walk away in two weeks and still be able to look at himself in a mirror he had to either show her she had nothing to worry about or help make her problems disappear. He could see only one way to do either, even though he hated to keep pushing it on her. Flexing the joints, he forced his fingers to relax. She hadn't dismissed the ghost VPN, simply stated she had no wish to use it. If he continued to push her he knew she'd say yes. In the end it would be for her own good.

"I was assured the RCMP will place your house on its regular patrols," he said.

"CSIS will no doubt be tapping my phone too, and watching for my passport at border crossings. None of that will help me sleep better at night." She stabbed a piece of lettuce with her fork. "On the bright side, imagine how much work I'll get done with all those extra waking hours."

Her words cut deep. She already knew the only conclusion she could reach was that she had no real alternative but to do what CSIS asked. The video suggested her situation had already begun to escalate. And while escalation would make CSIS become more actively involved, by the time they stepped up their game it might well be too late.

He wasn't about to stand back and allow anything to happen to her. He had two weeks to make sure nothing did.

Being asked to hack into the RBN wasn't what bothered Irina the most. Neither was the video—although that was bad enough on its own—or the discovery that CSIS was doing nothing to help her other than to provide a temporary babysitting service.

It was that, for the first time in her life, a gorgeous man had seemed genuinely interested in her for more than her mind. And what had she done?

Allowed it to cloud her normally sound judgment.

They couldn't be more different if they'd mailed in the specifications. She wasn't cut out for a life on the edge the way he clearly was. She didn't thrive on excitement. She'd almost passed out when she'd seen that video while he'd shrugged it off. The thought of hacking into the RBN made her heart race and her palms sweat whereas his face lit up like a child with a promising new toy. He wasn't always honest with her either. She might understand why he couldn't be, but realistically, it wouldn't be easy to live with. They were so, so wrong for each other.

And yet when he'd said two weeks a firestorm of conflicting emotions had erupted inside her. At some point, no doubt around 3 am when she'd been on top of him with her hands on his chest and her knees spanning his hips, she'd granted him a little too much access. She'd gotten emotionally involved and her emotional IQ wasn't on par with her intellect. The disparity left her floundering as to what to do next, although her instincts all screamed *retreat*. She wanted to hide in a cave and lick metaphorical wounds—self-inflicted no less.

"We both need to step back a bit," he was saying, echoing the direction her thoughts were taking. His next words suggested he might not necessarily be arriving at the same destination however. "Let's forget about all of this for a while. There's no rush for you to make a decision about the RBN. I invited you to go sightseeing and we're going sightseeing." He gestured at her plate with his fork. "Eat your lunch, babe. Let's go have some fun."

Fun was what had gotten them into this mess. In its pursuit they'd both lost track of what was important.

"Maybe it's time to face facts. Mixing business with..." She wanted to say pleasure but couldn't get the word out of her mouth. She was so hopeless at this, whatever it was. "Last night was my fault. I'm sorry about that," she finished, unable to meet his eyes. "With only two weeks left we need to focus on business."

He didn't answer right away. "We're dealing with two separate issues, here," he finally replied. "Whoever's doing this to you is trying to distract you and turn your attention from their real objective. That video's a diversion. And it's been a windfall for them, because let's face it, they weren't having a whole lot of luck without it. They don't know you reacted to the first pop-ups they sent you. You've been careful. We're all agreed they're after something though. We have to figure out what it might be. Finding out who's on the other side of the RBN is the simplest way. As for the second issue..." The heat in his eyes warmed her cheeks and she had no problem reading his mind. He shifted his legs. Under the table his shin brushed her bare calf. "We've got two weeks and we can't work around the clock." He waggled his brows, letting her know the physical contact wasn't accidental. "Let's stick with the original program. I'm in if you are."

Part of her wanted to say yes. She'd agreed to a short-term, casual sexual arrangement. It was what she'd wanted too. She'd thought she could do this. But the reality was much more complex than she'd anticipated and she wasn't used to this level of emotional upheaval. It was why she liked dealing with facts, not feelings, when making decisions.

If she'd gone with her feelings when she saw that video she'd be in jail for murder instead of sitting across from him having lunch.

"I'll think about it," she said.

His lips curved into a wicked, self-assured grin. "Oh, I have no doubt you will. You'll think it to death. You're wasting serious brain power by analyzing the inevitable, babe."

She ate her salad but turned down dessert. Once their bill was settled they took a tour of the winery, but her heart wasn't in it. She'd been looking forward to tonight. She wasn't any longer.

Their next stop was a point called the Look Off at the end of a steep winding road near the top of the North

Mountain. The blue sky was cloudless and the view across the valley nothing short of spectacular. Irina had lived in Nova Scotia for several years now and not once had she thought to come here. She was a little surprised that Kale had.

"What made you decide you had to see this?" she asked. She kept her gaze on the scenery spread out at her feet. "Don't tell me you've got a hang glider in the trunk of the car."

"I wish I'd thought to bring one."

The little-boy wistfulness had her rolling her eyes. "Oh, my God. You'd really do it, wouldn't you?"

"Of course. Look at that road and tell me it wouldn't be fun." He studied the path the asphalt cut through the trees as it curled up the mountain toward them. "This place would be perfect for longboarding, too."

"Do I dare ask what that is?"

"Skateboarding on steroids."

He couldn't be serious. "Even you wouldn't skateboard down a mountain."

"Of course not. I don't have a death wish. I haven't been on a skateboard in fifteen years. I'd have to get in some serious practice first. We'll come back next weekend."

"Are you out of—"

She stopped. He was teasing her. And as usual she'd taken the bait.

Before she could come up with a clever response another car pulled up beside theirs and a young family got out—tired-looking parents and four active small boys ranging in age from about one year to six or seven. Irina wasn't ruled by a ticking biological clock even though she was past thirty, but she still thought the boys were adorable.

The two oldest headed straight for the guard rail a few feet from where Irina and Kale were standing.

The oldest looked up at Kale, wary curiosity in his big brown eyes. "You're Iron Man's friend, aren't you?"

"Afraid not," Kale replied. "He's out of my league."

The boys groaned at what sounded like a joke—one Irina wasn't in on.

"Who's Iron Man?" she asked.

Both boys examined her. Their faces mirrored incredulity and quite possibly disgust.

"Don't mind her," Kale said to them. "She doesn't watch movies unless they have zombies in them." He shifted his attention to her. Blue eyes crinkled into a smile. "Iron Man is an Avenger. Everyone knows that."

She had only the vaguest idea what he was talking about. "Of course they do."

Kale shook his head in mock despair. "It's a good thing you're beautiful, babe. Your education might be fancy but it's far from well-rounded. We've got to pick up some DVDs on the way home."

The fact that Kale—so much larger than life in so many ways—saw her as beautiful and said it so casually, as if it were fact, both embarrassed and pleased her. She'd never based her opinion of herself on her appearance and was confident not many others did either. Until Kale came along she'd never cared.

He crouched down, making his size less intimidating to two awestruck little boys, and was soon deep in conversation with them. It struck her that he'd done a similar thing with her the first time they'd met. He'd taken a seat at the table so she wouldn't feel threatened.

When the father approached to reclaim his sons, Kale drew him into the discussion, too. The mother, about Irina's age, seemed shyer than the rest of her young family, trailing behind her husband with the baby on her hip and dragging a recalcitrant toddler by the hand. She cast Irina a friendly but hesitant smile as if to say, *"Men. What can you do?"* and Irina smiled back. She couldn't imagine having four children to care for, two of them still in diapers.

Watching Kale interact with the boys was another eye opener, making it even more difficult to believe he was a spy. *Inconspicuous* wasn't a word in his vocabulary. He attracted attention wherever he went, never bothering to try and blend in.

He glanced over and caught her staring at him. His eyebrows rose in a silent question. *What?*

She asked herself the same thing. The answer, so staggeringly unexpected, particularly in light of the day's prior events, caught her unprepared. Her heart began doing backflips. Then terror set in. This couldn't be happening. She was falling in love and with the least likely match. They only had one thing in common and who knew how long the great sex would last before he grew bored?

Her horror must have communicated itself and alarmed him, because the question she'd read in his eyes shifted to one of concern. He straightened. Past the loud background roar in her ears she heard him saying good-bye to the children and their parents. He wrapped an arm around her shoulders and steered her toward the car.

"Is something the matter?" he asked once they were back on the road, winding their way down the mountain. His lips quirked upward in humor. "I mean more than already?"

Her discovery changed nothing. Love was a purely psychological emotion. Even though they might wish for it, no one died of a broken heart.

Therefore the next words out of her mouth shocked her as much as they surprised him. They were rash and driven by nothing more than a desire to do something to impress him. To make her appear braver in his eyes than she really was. To walk a few yards in his shoes if hardly a mile.

"I'll do it," she said, her heart beating fast. "I'll hack into the RBN."

CHAPTER TWELVE

"NONE OF THIS MAKES any sense."

Irina stretched, her back and shoulder muscles aching. She'd been absorbed in her work for hours. While the ghost VPN had gotten her inside the RBN the trail it led her through was a long and convoluted one with dozens of intricate and questionable side paths that made her doubly careful about covering her tracks.

Kale set a cup of coffee on the table in front of her and pulled up a chair. He leaned over to peer at the screen, a solid wall of comfort and strength. She didn't like what she was doing and his physical presence stoked her bravery.

"What's the problem?" he asked.

"I've found a few possible places where my information might have landed, but there's so much other data coming through too. It all appears to be unrelated. Take this for instance." She showed him what she meant, shifting the laptop so he could get a better look. "This is credit card data coming in from an online shopping site. It has no connection to me or my work whatsoever."

Kale contemplated the screen, deep in thought, his lips a tight, unsmiling line, his forehead furrowed. Every inch of him vibrated with life, telling her how much he was loving all this. He enjoyed figuring out puzzles and connections and what made people tick, whereas she preferred dealing with cold, hard facts.

"You can't say for certain that it's unrelated," he disagreed. "We have no way of knowing who's using the information they're collecting, or what they're doing with it, or even if the information is really what it seems to be on the surface. Let's disregard the rest of it for now and focus on figuring out where yours is going."

She rubbed her tired eyes. "It's gone to at least three different places in two different countries."

"Those places have to have something in common other than you. Stick with your information. Have you thought about tracking any of the emails in your contact list to see if they're caught up in any of these threads you've found?"

While his suggestion had merit the task he proposed was a daunting one. "Where would I even start?"

"Your workplace. You have a few home emails from people in your office," he pointed out. "They're on your contact list too. Why not start with one of those?"

It was as good a place as any.

She returned to her keyboard. The first two email addresses she traced led her nowhere. They weren't used very often for anything other than communications with family. The third address, however, was a far different story. A hot bolt of incredulous fury shot through Irina. She double-checked it from both ends just to be sure. She didn't want to believe it, but the facts didn't lie. It led through the RBN to a second private address, and from there back to Irina's workplace.

And to Christine, the department's fresh-faced administrative assistant.

"Son of a bitch," Kale said when Irina showed him. "Talk about someone not being what she seems. How much are you willing to bet that she's your stalker too? Those pop-ups kept you distracted while she did her real work. That sex tape was genius."

Irina took a few deep breaths—in through her nose, out through her mouth—but it didn't help. She should have seen how it all fit together. "There's got to be some mistake. I don't understand why she'd do any of this."

Kale shrugged it off. "We've had this discussion already. Money. What else? I doubt very much if she's ideology driven, although again I'm making an assumption that will have to be investigated. My next assumption is that the online harassment was all a red herring to throw anyone off her real objective. For whatever reason, she—or someone else—wanted your personal email information. She already has access to your email at work. If she's as good as she appears to be she's most likely finagled access to your drone project too. Nothing's ever 100% secure." He raised his voice to a falsetto and batted his eyelashes, clasping his hands to his chest. "Please, Mr. Security Guy With Access To All The Right Keys. If I don't correct the filing mistake I made before mean, All-Mighty Dr. Glasov finds out about it, she'll have me fired. Her work is so *important*."

In spite of how angry she was and how violated she felt, the image Kale presented as he mimicked Christine made her laugh. Once she sobered and the first shock had passed she was able to think with her usual clarity again.

"Of what possible value could my private email be to her?"

"Not to her. Whoever she sold it to," Kale corrected her. He tapped the edge of her laptop's keyboard. "Now we need to find out who that is and where your mutual trails converge." He dropped a kiss on her forehead. "Get back to work, babe. The clock is ticking."

A few hours later, in the wee hours of the morning, she finally found the connection. Kale was asleep on the sofa in the next room, so she went to wake him to give him the news.

She flipped a table lamp on and reached out to place her hand on his shoulder, then drew it back. Once they verified her information, and confirmed the identity of the person harassing her, there'd be no need for Kale to stay any longer—not even for the two weeks he'd assured her he'd been given.

Two weeks would change nothing other than make it harder for her heart to let him go. Wistfulness tugged at it even now as she watched him sleep, a white throw pillow tucked beneath his blond head and one long leg hanging off the cushions so that his bare foot rested flat on the floor. Why couldn't he have been a linguistics professor? Or the rumpled, affable, unemployed, kite-surfing gym teacher he'd pretended to be?

She'd be fine either way.

But a spy...

While her fears for her physical safety had largely dissipated now that the threat was no longer faceless, the reality was, Irina hadn't liked the stress and uncertainty of the past few weeks. She hated being caught up in espionage, online or otherwise. Those things were part of Kale's world, not hers, and he lived for them. He'd made no secret of where his loyalties resided either. He'd want to pass what she'd found with the VPN on to his boss, and sooner rather than later.

She shook his shoulder. He was awake in an instant, sitting upright and blinking the sleep from his eyes.

"You aren't going to believe this," she said to him.

"Christine's personal email traffic and the information the botnet stole off my computer all ended up in Ottawa. In the Ministry of Defence office no less."

Kale's face registered shock as the significance sank in.

"Holy shit."

And wasn't that a complete understatement?

Irina showed him what she'd found, explaining it to him as simply as she could with him doing his best to keep up. He might speak five languages, but he'd flunked out of geek.

"Any chance you're mistaken?" he asked, although without any real hope.

She gave him that pokered-up, disbelieving, Dr. Glasov stare and shook her head. "You're looking at the same results I am."

Maybe so. But he didn't understand them even half so well. Man, she was smart.

"Since I'm using a VPN supplied by CSIS to hack into a Canadian government site, I didn't dare go any farther," she was continuing, unaware she'd left him miles behind. "That can't be legal."

Hell, no. It was not.

"I've got to make a phone call," he said.

Seconds later he had a sleepy, very cross Dan on the line.

"What couldn't wait two hours until morning?" his team leader growled. "If the doctor is pregnant that's your sorry-ass problem and I don't want to hear about it. Not now and not ever."

Kale hoped Irina hadn't heard any of that. He half turned away from her, switching the phone to his other ear. "You're still a dick, Dan. And if I'd waited two hours to tell you what Irina found out you'd have me shot."

Dan listened without interrupting as Kale filled him in.

"I take it all back," he said once Kale was done. "I'd rather hear how you two are naming your first born after me." There was another long stretch of silence that Kale waited out. "Here's what we're going to do. Dr. Glasov is going to file a harassment complaint against the admin assistant for the porn tape. We'll get the assistant fired and out of a position where she has access to government information." He cut off Kale's protest. "Dr. Glasov is going to have to suck up any embarrassment she'll suffer. Let's not tip anyone in Ottawa off that the admin assistant's RBN activity has been traced. There are bigger, more important fish to go after, here."

"Understood." Kale hoped Irina would too, because she'd done CSIS a favor and this was her thanks.

"And Martin?"

"Yes?"

"You probably think I'm being a complete shit right now, but you should know that one of the names on the email list you gave me is a nuclear physicist who turned up dead in London yesterday morning. It's being reported by the press as a heart attack, but our intelligence claims it was an assassination. Happened right outside his hotel room door. Someone was waiting for him. He was working on the drone project too."

Irina was watching Kale so he worked hard to keep his reaction off his face, but he couldn't stop his hands from shaking.

"Do you think there'll be any more incidents like this?" he asked carefully.

"Meaning is Dr. Glasov's life in danger? We don't think so, no. While she's designing the weapons systems placement on the drone project, this guy was building the actual weapon. The CIA's had an interest in him for a while too, so it's unlikely he was an innocent bystander. The director believes the physicist's name was cross-referenced against Dr. Glasov's email list simply to confirm he was the hit they needed to make. It might or might not have something to do with that drone—either way, we don't want anyone, including the CIA, tipped off that Canada is now investigating. Whoever Dr. Glasov's company is building this drone for it won't be the actual end customer and we want to know who that end customer is. This is why we have to keep that admin assistant from figuring out she's been caught distributing a lot more than pornography. You have until Friday to finish up things with Dr. Glasov and get that admin assistant out of her office," Dan added. "And be sure to pass on our thanks to her for cracking the RBN for us. But don't tell her the truth about the nuclear physicist's death."

"What happened to the two weeks you gave me?"

"I'm taking them back. I really need you in London right now. I wish you'd been there six days ago. Why should the CIA have all the fun?"

Kale disconnected the call. The truth about Irina's colleague's death wasn't information he'd ever share. He didn't want her to find out that someone she knew had been assassinated, and probably thanks in part to information stolen from her. She'd take ownership of it.

He also wished he had more than five days to confirm she wasn't in any danger. It was easy enough for Dan to shrug off. He'd never met her. He wasn't involved.

"Dan says to say thanks."

"Tell him I'm overwhelmed by his gratitude." Irina's hands balled into fists at her sides, morphing into a familiar, irate little pixie with three pencil stubs sticking out of her untidy knot of hair, too cute for words. If she had any questions about that two week comment he'd made she wasn't letting on. Instead, as usual, she focused on what was important. "What happens after Christine is arrested?"

Kale cursed Dan some more for leaving him to be the bearer of bad news, then bucked up his courage. Irina was the most reasonable and logical woman he knew. She always seemed able to work through her emotions and grasp the big picture.

"About that," he began, ill at ease and fighting hard to hide it. Lying to her didn't come as easily anymore. "She's not going to be arrested." He explained the problems it would create if she were. Irina kept nodding, seeming to be in complete agreement with Dan's line of thinking. Encouraged by her understanding thus far Kale dropped the bomb. "We do, however, need to get her away from any further access to government information. You need to file a harassment complaint against her so we can get her fired."

It took Irina all of three seconds to figure out the problem with that. "And admit to the entire senior management team that it's me in that video?" Her voice trembled with anger, the outrage behind it making him wince. She had a right to feel she'd been betrayed. "No. They'll want to review it to confirm they have just cause to dismiss her. They'll know I circumvented their security measures to try and hide the video too. This will ruin my career—or at the very least my credibility."

"Whether you go to senior management or CSIS does, they're going to find out about the video sooner or later.

And yes, they'll want to watch it." Kale didn't dare delve any further into their possible reasons behind that curiosity either. She was angry enough without feeling completely exploited. "The only difference is that if CSIS has to officially report what you found about the Ministry of Defence connection it will compromise an already ongoing investigation into national security."

"I'm caring less and less about national security by the second. When does *my* security come into play?" she demanded.

And then she was blinking back tears.

He rubbed the back of his neck. This whole day had derailed on him. He'd wanted to take her out. Let her get to know him as more than the government agent currently invading her space. Instead she'd been dragged into doing work that walked a tad south of the finer lines of the law. She'd been lied to, then thrown under the bus. To top it all off he wasn't good with crying women. He hated the feeling of helplessness it always gave him.

But it was almost five in the morning and she'd had her second big shock in less than twenty-four hours. A reaction like this was long overdue, so he did the only thing he could think of, which was to wrap her in his arms and hope like hell it made her feel safe and secure.

His hope was short-lived. She turned into a tight ball of tension.

"I wonder if this is being caught on video too," she said, her tone dripping sarcasm.

The living room curtains were open. He hadn't wanted to keep them drawn all the time, possibly tipping anyone off that the camera had been discovered. Now it no longer mattered.

Her reaction, however, provided him with another insight into her complex character. The thought of being caught in a moment of weakness wasn't any more acceptable to her than being videotaped in a sex act.

Or maybe she was simply too exhausted to get her priorities straight.

He switched off the lamp, plunging the room into that thin gloom of morning before the sun rose and the street lights winked out. "I can remove the camera right now if you'd like," he offered.

"It doesn't matter. I'm going to bed."

She twisted out of his arms, putting her words into action, but he wasn't about to let her leave in this uncharacteristically dark mood. She sounded not just tired but defeated and he couldn't allow that. Not when he was responsible for it. He caught her elbow. "Couples rules, remember? Never go to bed angry."

"I shouldn't have to keep pointing this out. We aren't a couple. Couples rules don't apply. Besides, I'm not angry with you."

She was a terrible liar. Right now she was so pissed she couldn't even look at him. She was also wrong if she thought they weren't a couple. It might not be a permanent arrangement, but he'd never had this kind of relationship—whatever this was—with any woman before. He wasn't going to suddenly stop caring about her. Therefore, in his books, this counted and those rules applied. "I don't like to see you upset."

"Then you should have thought of that before you asked me to do CSIS's dirty work for them."

His blood pressure took a sharp upward spike. He couldn't allow that jagged-edged barb to go unchallenged. He believed in the work he did. It wasn't always pretty, it was rarely straightforward, and often there was no happy ending. He knew it and had to live with it. She didn't get to ignore the fallout from the type of work she did either.

"You're a smart woman, Irina. You didn't do it because I asked you to. You did it because it needed to be done."

Her chin tilted upward, eyes wide, indecipherable pools in the semi-dark room. "Is that what you think?"

Well, yes. But the sudden stillness to her expression made him a whole lot less certain of it.

She shook her elbow free of his grip. "And I thought you were a smart man. It looks like we were both wrong tonight."

She'd done it for him.

Blindsided, his blood pressure leveled off and his gut took a plunge. Until this very second he'd had no reason to consider that he might mean much to her beyond her personal safety and a warm body for sex. Even though he knew she liked him—hell, he liked her too—it didn't take a genius to figure out they were both more wrapped up in their careers than they were in each other.

But if she'd hacked into the RBN because he'd asked it of her, it cast their friendly relationship in a whole different light, and if she wanted to take things to the next level, then he was on board. He was heading to London in a few days. She'd be in Paris in a few weeks. They both traveled a lot. A long distance, casual relationship— friends with benefits, so to speak—might well suit them both.

An exclusive one though. She didn't get to talk dirty science with anyone else.

He followed her into the hall and stuck out a hand before she could close her bedroom door. "You don't get to walk away in the middle of a disagreement," he said. "I have a few things I'd like to say too."

She crossed her arms over her chest. "I'm listening."

He leaned against the door frame, refusing to enter her private sanctum without the invitation he wanted. "That's part of the problem, babe. You listen, but you don't always hear. I blame your fancy degrees."

She put a few extra feet of distance between them. "You bring up my education a lot. You have advanced degrees of your own, don't forget."

"And I use them to pay attention to what's going on. For example." He looked around the room, examining each piece of furniture before once again settling his gaze on her. "Do you know how long I've been hinting around for you to invite me in here?"

"The sofa, the hall, and the spare room weren't enough? What difference could using my bed possibly make?" She looked bewildered, but he wasn't buying it. She had to have known. She'd been too careful about keeping him out.

"Oh, it makes a big difference," he assured her. She was rubbing her arms now, a sure sign he'd struck a nerve, so he applied a little more pressure. "You need to pay attention to people, Irina. What am I saying to you?"

Her eyes slid away from his. "I never have any idea what you're talking about."

No way was he letting her get away with that tired excuse. "Yes you do."

"Fine." She brought her gaze back to his face, biting the inside of her lip. "This is my private space and I don't want you in it."

He continued to push. "Why not?"

Her lower lip trembled. "Because I want one room in my house where I won't be reminded of you. Are you happy now?"

He was the furthest thing from it. She'd heard him ask Dan about those two weeks and realized he wasn't going to be here as long as he'd planned on. "So once I'm gone you never plan to think about me again?"

"Do you plan to think about me?" she fired back.

"Every damn day. But we both knew going into this that our careers demand a lot of our time." He took a deep breath before plunging ahead. He'd never offered a woman this level of commitment before. "That doesn't mean we can't keep in touch. We have one thing in common and you've got admit, it's pretty spectacular. We can always pick up where we leave off whenever we're in the same city."

She didn't leap into his arms, wrap her legs around him, and scream *yes*. Her bottom lip, however, stopped trembling. Dr. Glasov reappeared.

"I'll sleep on it," she said with that calm, professional politeness that always intimidated the hell out of him and at the same time turned him on. "In the meantime you can use your own fancy degrees and intelligence training to figure out what I'm saying to you, since you always pay such close attention."

She shut the door in his face. He heard the gentle but firm click of the lock.

Well, that sound was easy enough for him to understand.

CHAPTER THIRTEEN

"WHAT I DO IN the privacy of my home is my business."

Irina had requested this meeting with the director of Human Resources for eleven o'clock. It was now almost noon, meaning she'd been answering questions for the better part of an hour, and mentally she was exhausted. Her stomach quivered like jelly and she knew her face had to be as red as the cranberry carpet. There was no avoiding the humiliation of this.

Fortunately the director of Human Resources was professional. A trim, fifty-something woman wearing black-framed glasses and a pale pink business suit, she radiated a kind but no-nonsense demeanor. If she had an opinion on the whole matter she wasn't letting it show.

"I know that, Dr. Glasov. But this is a serious complaint. No one is questioning why you chose to track down the origins of that video yourself. Under the circumstances it's perfectly understandable." A smile briefly flickered. "While they'll never admit it you probably saved the IT department a lot of time and a massive headache." The smile slid away. "You do realize, of course, that we'll require that video as proof, as well as the information on how you were able to track it to her?"

Irina nodded. She'd already filtered the details so the path to Christine was more direct, omitting the RBN and Ottawa connections. The director continued her gentle probing. "I can't imagine what reason someone you say you barely know would have for harassing you in such a manner. Can you think of any?"

"None."

Kale had done some digging and passed on a little of what he'd found out. Christine's former college roommate was a Liberian woman who'd been studying in Canada and now lived in the Netherlands, working as an engineer for a company specializing in port construction. The Liberian's connections were murkier and would involve CSIS discussions with Interpol to sort out, because they crossed several international boundaries. Kale said his boss believed the Liberian—through Christine—was after information about the drone's end user too. Why, they didn't know. Neither did they know why Christine's cyber trail led to the Canadian Ministry of Defence office. It wasn't information they'd share with Irina even if they did discover the connection.

She stood, beyond ready for this meeting to be over. "Thank you for your time, but I'll have to leave the matter in your hands. I have a lunch appointment in the city and I'm going to be late."

She'd called her friend Beverley right after contacting Human Resources and asked if she were free any time that day. Since Bev had to be at a working group session in the downtown area of the city all week they were having lunch at a trendy pub popular with the local business crowd.

Once she was outside, Irina breathed deeply of the fresh air and sunshine and tried to let go of the tension. The HR offices were across the street from her building, with the parking lot between them, so she wouldn't have to go back to her office again and risk running into Christine.

She planned to play hooky the rest of the day. She'd refused to allow Kale to drive her to work that morning, so for the first time in weeks she had her car and her freedom. She'd pointed out to him that, if she no longer had a reason to be worried about her safety, then there was no need for him to act as her chauffeur. He'd chosen not to argue. Lucky for him.

Pick up where we leave off...

He hadn't argued when his boss took those extra two weeks from him either. From *them*. Anger coiled inside her, a snake poised and ready but with nowhere to strike. She couldn't say who she was angriest with—Kale or herself. She'd gone into a sexual relationship willingly. He wasn't to blame for how it turned out. He had no idea how she felt about it or him.

But he should.

The insensitive bastard.

There were no empty meters to be found on the street when Irina reached the city so she left her car at a local parkade and walked the few blocks to Durty Nelly's. A light, humid breeze off Halifax Harbour left the city sweltering in a late summer heat wave. The steep upward climb and her impractical high heels made her late. She arrived breathless and sticky, her hairline damp at the nape of her neck.

Beverley waited for her at a table in a corner of the outdoor patio, patiently eyeing the men walking by on the sidewalk from under the shade of an umbrella. Irina slid into a chair, the green plastic hot against the backs of her legs. She'd be sticking to it in no time.

"To what do I owe this unexpected pleasure?" Bev

asked. "I'm going to go out on a limb and guess it has something to do with the incredibly gorgeous new man in your life."

"I don't know where to begin."

"Tell Doctor Bev all about it. Let's start with the bedroom. That's the root of all evil."

They placed their lunch orders while Irina gathered her nerve. She grabbed the sweating glass of lemon water the waitress left her and took a long swallow. Her throat had gone painfully dry. She set the half-empty glass on her paper napkin to keep it from blowing away.

"I filed a harassment complaint against the administrative assistant in my office this morning," she blurted out.

"Wow." Bev sat back in her chair. "I did not see that coming."

"Neither did I."

Irina stuck with the story she'd agreed to tell Human Resources. Bev, of all people, would understand how humiliating and potentially career damaging this was for her.

No one else did. Rather no one else cared.

"A sex tape...I don't know if I should be congratulating you or offering my sympathy," Bev said when she'd finished. "I'm going to focus on the positive and go with congratulations."

Irina couldn't believe it. "You see something positive in this?"

"I see you coming out of your comfort zone. Your safe little shell. You're a young, attractive woman, Irina. Life is passing you by. Embarrassment isn't going to kill you. Even if it did at least you'd die with a little fun under your chastity belt."

"I have a life."

"You have a career," Bev corrected her. "You work all the time. And most of the time it isn't very much fun."

That wasn't true. The only fun Irina'd had lately was thanks in large part to her career, although she couldn't confide that particular tidbit of information to her friend. Kale was the only person she could share secrets with that were both professional and personal. Unfortunately, right now he featured highly in both.

"You don't think I should be worried?" Irina asked, incredulous. She'd expected commiseration, not censure.

"You should be, yes. But ten years from now it's not going to make any difference. You're respected for your mind. That's all the scientific community really cares about. If that video is as murky in detail as you say it is, then the majority of them are going to choose to believe it's not you. Only a few people you work with right now will know the difference and they're hardly about to make a public announcement. A security breach looks bad on them. And if word about the video does get out all you have to do is sit back and neither confirm nor deny."

Out of the corner of her eye, Irina caught sight of a man walking up the street toward Durty Nelly's. He was talking on a cell phone. She turned her head to watch him, trying to figure out where she'd seen him before. The pulse throbbed in her throat. That day at the beach. The man Kale hadn't liked. He was dressed in a suit and tie, not a wetsuit, which was why it took her so long to place him.

His eyes slid right on past. He didn't recognize her. Why would he? Here, she was simply one of many professional women having lunch, most of them more attractive and noteworthy than she was. She didn't stand out from the crowd.

Her pulse steadied again. She turned back to Bev and the topic of their conversation.

"Do you really believe it's that simple?" She hardly dared hope it was true.

"I do." Their lunches arrived. Bev took a bite of her salad. "While there aren't any sex tapes in my past that I know of, I've had my fair share of professional embarrassments. FYI—having an affair with your married boss gets noticed. And quit looking so shocked. It was a long time ago when I was fresh out of college. I learned from my mistakes. You will too. Next time pull the curtains. And also for future reference, always lock the office door."

Irina laughed. It felt good.

It didn't, however, resolve her anger with Kale, which she couldn't seem to get past. All she had to do was tell him she wasn't interested in what he proposed and yet she couldn't bring herself to do it.

After lunch, the two women parted ways on the sidewalk in front of the pub.

Bev had to return to her working group. Irina, however, who had the afternoon off, was in no particular rush to go home and face Kale.

Her high heels weren't meant for walking, limiting her entertainment options. A hike farther up the steep streets to visit the Public Gardens was out. Traipsing through boutiques held little appeal. Besides, she preferred doing her shopping online. That left the waterfront where she could sit on a bench in the shade and watch the ships come and go in the harbor.

She walked the short distance downhill to the boardwalk and spent an hour on a bench before growing bored. She couldn't avoid Kale forever. She also had a conference presentation she'd like to finish. Paris was six weeks away.

She'd left her car on the third level of the parkade. The tap of her heels on the steps echoed loudly. Her toes ached. The afternoon heat hadn't yet seeped past the concrete walls of the outer stairwell, leaving them dank and smelling of urine. It was three o'clock, that period of time when visitors had already headed out of the city to beat the afternoon traffic, but before the workday was finished, leaving the parkade empty of people.

When she reached the first landing and turned to take the next flight of stairs a soft noise caught her attention. She paused to listen, but the sound wasn't repeated. She started up the next flight.

The noise came again. Disconcerted, she stopped. So did the sound. She reached in her purse for her car key and her cell phone. She punched in 911 but didn't hit send. She kept the phone in one hand and her key in the other as she continued to climb. She didn't hurry her steps and she didn't stop to listen again. If someone was following her there was no purpose in letting them know she was aware of their presence.

The footsteps below her were unmistakable now and gathering speed. The heavier tread and the softer ring of the shoes on the stairs indicated it was a man. She reached the level where she'd parked her car and pushed through the swinging doors. The lot was full of cars but empty of people. Hers was on the far side of the parkade from the stairs. She didn't want to look foolish, or worse scared, by sprinting for her car. Her high heels weren't practical for that purpose anyway. She did, however, glance at her watch and quicken her pace as if she were late for an appointment.

She wished Kale were here.

"Dr. Glasov, wait up," someone called.

She stopped and turned back to the doors leading to the stairwell. She couldn't catch her breath. It was the man from the beach again.

Her thumb remained firmly in position on the send button of her phone. If all he wanted was to speak with her he could have done so at the pub. While there was a slight chance he'd only just recognized her, he had no reason to follow her up the stairs in such a furtive and frightening manner. The possibility that he'd happened to park in the same garage—and on the same floor—was even less likely. Neither did she recall giving him her name. She doubted very much if Kale would have done so.

And Kale hadn't liked him. That was the biggest red flag. If he tried to come too close, or did anything she found threatening, she was pressing that button.

She again looked at her watch, masking nervousness with the impatience she reserved for competitors who thought to make names by discrediting her work. "I'm late for a meeting."

He stopped two parking spaces from her. Irina could place a parked car between them if she had to. He put his hands in the air. "I have a message for you to pass on to your friend for me." He remained pleasant enough, but there was an edginess to it that Irina found frightening. He took a step closer. "Tell him he might not be stupid easy to find, but his friends are."

This wasn't about her, then. It was about getting at Kale. Blind rage overcame any fear. He wanted to threaten a CSIS intelligence officer?

He could do it in person.

Irina's thumb hit the send button. She held up her phone. A bored voice, loud in the empty, echoing parkade, crackled, *"911, where is your emergency?"*

Angry red blotches mottled the man's throat and cheeks. "What the hell are you doing?"

She gave the police dispatcher the parkade address.

Then, before he could recover from his surprise, she snapped his picture.

"Crazy bitch."

For a heart-pounding second she thought he might grab for her phone. She read the intent in his eyes.

Instead, he took off for the doors to the stairwell, not running, but walking very fast.

For her part Irina made a mad dash for her car, unmindful of her precarious heels, aching toes, and the undignified spectacle she undoubtedly made.

She locked herself inside the vehicle and waited for the police to arrive.

Kale couldn't remember the last time he'd come this close to losing his shit. A man of his size, in his line of work, either learned self-control or faced unemployment.

Right now, despite Irina being safe and sound in her kitchen and standing in front of him, trying to keep all that anger in check left his brain on the verge of implosion. As near as he could ascertain the investment banker had spotted her at Durty Nelly's—of all places—and followed her to a parking garage to deliver a threat. Kale shook his head. People with that level of entitled arrogance were naïve and stupid. He was so sure his friends could protect him that he'd gotten overconfident. A little flattery from the right sources had convinced him he was invincible. He wasn't. While he'd done nothing to Irina to get him arrested, it was coming—and thanks to his actions today there'd be no cutting deals for him when it did. His terrorist buddies would be the first ones to let him swing too.

But Irina was trying to pretend that what happened to her was nothing to be concerned about and that wasn't OK. She wasn't invincible either. While she'd had the presence of mind to call 911, and Kale applauded her for it, taking the guy's picture stepped over the line. Cold sweat chilled his skin and his soul. If it had been one of the banker's friends following her instead and she'd pulled that stunt, the outcome of this afternoon might have been far, far different. They had zero fear of the law.

He pulled his shit together long enough to ask the question that bugged him the most. "Why didn't you call me?"

"What good would that have done?"

She sounded so calm. So practical. And she was right. There wasn't a thing he could have done to help and that scared him even more. He tracked down terrorists. An element of danger was inherent in his line of work. While he accepted that for himself, and truthfully, maybe enjoyed it a little more than he should, a threat to someone close to him was a nightmare come true.

She rinsed the potatoes she'd peeled, then carefully cut them in chunks before seasoning them and wrapping them in tinfoil. She set the tidy packets on a tray. "Would you start these on the barbecue for me? Steaks are up next."

He didn't pick up the tray. Now that his anger wasn't affecting his reasoning, a few holes in her story jumped out at him. She should have been in her office all day. If he'd known she intended to go elsewhere he'd have insisted on driving. "Why were you in the city and not at work?"

She began shredding a head of lettuce for a salad, dropping leafy handfuls into a spinner sitting in the sink. "I told you. I was having lunch with Beverley."

He didn't buy her explanation. It was a break in routine

and that was unlike her. "Why today, all of a sudden?"

"What makes you think it was all of a sudden?"

"Because it wasn't in your day planner." He confessed to snooping through her agenda without shame. His job was to gather information. What he did to obtain it was offset by its value. In this case it was priceless. Or should have been.

She tackled dicing the green peppers with unwarranted ferocity. A tendril of hair clung to the slender line of her throat, curling gently against a bare shoulder. "Neither was the appointment I had with HR. You can pass on to your boss that Christine is going to be fired tomorrow if you'd like."

This day continued to dole out surprises. He'd known Irina would file the complaint because it was the right thing to do, but never dreamed she'd do it so soon or without more prodding from him. He would have preferred to finesse the script they'd agreed on. "How did it go?"

"As well as expected. Maybe a little less humiliating in that the director of HR is a woman."

"Good for you, always looking for the silver lining," he said.

Thinning lips and an expressive roll of those sea-green eyes indicated her lack of appreciation for his half-assed and ill-timed attempt at a joke. She wasn't as unaffected by today's events as she tried to pretend.

Neither was he. A hard fist of guilt pounded his chest. He'd brought this to her door. He wanted so badly to hold her. Instead he grabbed the tray and took it outside on the patio where the barbecue awaited.

Sultry heat from the late afternoon sun blanketed the tiny back yard. Crickets chirped in the dry grass along the edge of the ragged birch trees. He dragged in a lungful of air laden with the scent of vanilla from pyeweed bordering the fence and grabbed a few seconds to think it all through. Calling the police first was the right decision for her to make and in line with her way of thinking. But he hadn't been her second call either, and it was hard to ignore the reason why not. He'd thought she might be falling for him, but mounting evidence suggested that even if she were she was far too smart to invest her heart in someone she couldn't rely on.

He hadn't been nearly as clever. His heart was invested in her all right. And right now it was twisted in tight, painful knots. The next three days were going to be hell, but the thought of heading to London before sorting out the personal problems between them didn't sit well.

He opened the propane valve underneath the barbecue and pressed the ignite switch on the front, then arranged the packets of foil-wrapped potatoes on the lower grill. He'd move them to the top when it was time to cook the steak.

Inside the house, through the half-open sliding patio door that led to the kitchen, he could hear Irina moving between the fridge and the island. Today could have ended in disaster, but thankfully it hadn't. Relief wound its way from his feet to his head, edging out the last bits of anger and fear, leaving him dizzy and counting his blessings. She'd remained her usual calm, controlled, rational self. The investment banker was probably already in the backseat of a police cruiser, demanding to speak to his lawyer. The admin assistant was about to be fired, which hopefully would make her online activities a lot easier to trace. Without her government clearances she'd have no high-security servers to hide behind. A thorough background check had confirmed money problems but no history of radicalism or violence. Interpol had nothing on her.

Well. They'd had nothing on her before. They did now.

Leaving Kale with three days to end things on a better note with Irina. She might not plan to pick up where they left off if they ever ended up in the same city again, but this was the present and they hadn't left off anything yet.

He was selfish enough to want her to remember him, but for the right reasons and not this current parade of disasters.

CHAPTER FOURTEEN

THEY LINGERED OVER WINE on the patio after dinner, with citronella candles burning in a circle around them to ward off the mosquitoes, because once the sun settled below the treetops, the bloodthirsty little beggars came out in full force.

Kale fiddled with his cell phone, pretending to check for messages while he struggled to find some neutral topic of conversation. His knees bumped the underside of the round teakwood bistro table. The matching teak deck chair, while sturdy, was a size too small for him and it creaked under his fidgeting weight.

He topped off their glasses from the half-empty wine bottle between them. Irina had been quiet all through their meal and he hated not knowing what was going on in her head. With any other woman he would have been out the door long before things grew this awkward. Instead the flight to London on Friday loomed over his head like a hurricane at sea.

Maybe it was time they discussed it. Then they could get back to making the best of the time they had left together.

"Could you give me a lift to the airport on Friday?" he asked.

"Friday?" Her self-possession slipped a fraction, a good indication that maybe he should have finessed his question a little better. A frown formed, accompanied by a flash of distress in her eyes. "Where are you going?" She held up her hand, palm out, then reached for her wine and took a long sip before returning the glass to the table. "Sorry, that's CSIS business. Forget I asked."

He didn't care if she knew where he was. There was no need for her to worry. No one was going to torture the information out of her. "London. I don't know how long I'll be there."

She'd be in Paris in a few weeks, he would have loved to add, and point out it was a short hop by plane. But let her come to that conclusion herself.

Night was settling around them, holding a faint trace of approaching fall on its edges. Her slight frown reappeared. "Does it ever bother you, not knowing where you're going to be from one week to the next?"

She had to be kidding. His was the best job in the world. "Not a bit. Sitting in an office all day would make me want to hang myself."

She rolled her eyes. "I picked up on that. The surfing and mountain longboarding tipped me off. But don't you ever think about your future?"

"Rarely," he admitted. "I'm happy with where I am right now."

And yet that wasn't one hundred percent true anymore. While he'd been happy with his life a month or so ago she'd thrown off his game, and now for her own personal reasons, she didn't want to stay in contact with him. He wouldn't push her on that decision. She had a right to lead her life the way she saw fit too. Give them a few weeks and they'd both be back right where they belonged.

Those thoughts didn't give him the comfort they

should. "What about you?" He turned his chair so that his legs were no longer under the table and rested one ankle on the opposite knee, getting more comfortable and prepared to lighten the mood. Riling Dr. Glasov never grew old. "We both know you've got your life mapped out until well into your nineties, Dr. Babe."

Her lush lips puckered into a pixie pout. "I still hate you calling me that." She stared into space. "And I don't have my life completely mapped out. There are too many variables to consider. At some point I hope to work fulltime as an independent consultant. I'd like to teach too, and write a few more books."

"But you'll want a family someday."

Envisioning cute little brown-haired pixie children with pale, pretty green eyes punched him straight in the feels. Picturing someone else as their father was a knee in the nuts. Of course she would want kids. She was a thirty-two year old woman with a biological clock. It stood to reason that she'd want something permanent from their father in terms of a relationship too.

He, on the other hand, wasn't ready for white picket fences and a rocking chair on a porch with a view of the sunset. The prospect gave him heart palpitations. While he'd never say never he wasn't handing out false hope.

But he'd enjoyed the past few weeks with Irina and the quiet moments like this. She was a port in a storm. A serene lagoon surrounded by a barrier reef keeping the wild ocean at bay. Except when it came to the bedroom...

He edged his bare foot forward so it touched the tip of her toe while his eyes dipped into the valley of her low-cut cropped top, enjoying the view of her breasts. She might well hang out with the world's finest minds and be highly respected for hers, but she still had no idea how sexy she was or how much power it gave her over him. Heaven help him if she ever figured it out.

Her gaze was clear, cool, and direct, bringing him back to earth. "You mean because all women have biological clocks? While possibly true, some of us aren't driven by them. I don't have any plans for a family. If it happens it happens. But I do know that if it does, children are a shared responsibility and deserve two parents who are committed to them."

Meaning their father wouldn't be someone like him. Kale got the message and he was in complete agreement. That didn't mean it made him happy.

So much for lightening the mood.

She kicked back her chair and picked up her empty glass. "I'm going to do dishes."

He gathered his too, and the now empty wine bottle, and followed her into the kitchen, sliding the screen to the patio door shut behind him but leaving the glass section open to let in the night air. She shouldered past him, pushing him out of her way as she moved between the dishwasher and the island, and he grinned at a spontaneous recollection of the first time they'd met right here in this room. She might never be able to use a knife as a weapon, or physically defend herself, but she was no half-witted female who wandered into the basement wearing her best lingerie to check out strange noises either. She'd done everything right today. She assessed situations and took appropriate action.

And even when he knew he shouldn't, he couldn't seem to resist doing whatever it took to shake all that reserve.

He stepped up behind her and slid an arm around her waist, bending to press his lips to her cheek. He dragged a fingertip along the length of her clavicle, appreciating the fineness of its structure while watching her shiver. Her breath quickened, chasing away the air of indifference toward him she tried to present. She closed her eyes, her thoughts disappearing behind her dark lashes. She couldn't as easily hide her desire.

She didn't need him, no. Neither was she interested in what he offered in terms of a relationship, which granted, wasn't much. She did, however, still want him in at least one respect. So he wasn't the man of her dreams. Why couldn't he at least be a great memory for her to take out and look back on with fondness?

He slid one hand up her belly to cup her breast beneath her skimpy top. She stretched, arching her back so her shoulders pressed against his chest and her buttocks his groin. She tipped her head to the side, exposing her throat. He trailed his lips from the crook of her shoulder to her ear, taking the lobe between his teeth and giving it a light nip. Her hands moved behind her to his hips. She turned her face so that her mouth met his lips.

"Open your eyes," he coaxed her. "Tell me what you're thinking."

Two jewels gazed back at him, examining him in return. "That the dishes can wait until morning."

She had such a dry sense of humor. Everything about her made him ache to sink himself inside of her. But, as tempting as it was to bend her over the island and take her right there, tonight maybe he'd try a different approach. While sex was the one area of her life where she needed very little encouragement—something that never failed to amaze him—and there was nothing wrong with slowing things down and thinking them through, tonight he'd do the thinking for both of them. He'd make her put that beautiful brain in neutral and let go of a really bad day.

He scooped her into his arms and headed for the bedroom. She crooked her elbow around his neck. He didn't slow down at her door, but nudged it wide with his foot and swung her into the room. Lingering twilight spilled through the open window. A few long strides carried him across the carpet. He tossed her—gently—onto the pillows, then shucked out of his shorts while she watched. The T-shirt followed.

"Do you still want to know what I'm thinking?" she asked as he stretched out beside her.

He rested his elbow on the blankets and propped his head in his hand to stare down at her. "Nah. You're thinking of me."

"Oh, I am," she assured him, her tone giving him no clue as to where this conversation was headed, and he tensed, well aware he was on shaky ground by bringing her here. "But I'm also wondering why it's so important to you that you sleep in my bed."

Because he wanted to make certain she thought of him whenever she crawled between the smooth sheets. He wanted to be able to think of her at night and picture her asleep in this very bed and pretend she was dreaming of him. He wanted to ruin it for anyone else. "It's queen-sized."

She didn't call him on the lie. A soft, resigned sigh was the only indicator she gave that she knew better than to believe him, which made him smile. For someone supposedly brilliant she could be gullible sometimes. But not right now.

"You've had a hard day, Dr. Babe. Let me help you relax."

He stretched her hands above her head, then peeled her frayed denim shorts off her slender legs, kissing the insides of her thighs as he bared them. She gave a soft gasp, clenching her fingers into tight little fists. The panties she wore weren't her usual thong he noted straight off. Seemed she'd needed more courage today. Remorse pinched his heart. They were lacy, and covered her from hip to thigh, but the black lace was so sheer that the coverage was all an illusion.

"Mercy," he breathed. That earned him a smile. He sat back on his heels and looked his fill, from the scrap of sheer lace to the exposed skin of her midriff, to the cropped hem of the top he'd had his hands under so he already knew she wasn't wearing a bra. "If you ever do take up teaching I'm heading back to school."

Her eyebrows went up and she pursed her full lips. The bed creaked as she shifted her hips, signaling she was already restless and anxious for him to proceed. "Has someone been bad? Does the teacher need to give him a spanking?"

He almost came right there. That was unexpected. "I'm willing to give it due consideration another time. Tonight I thought we'd take things in a different direction. Do you trust me?"

She didn't hesitate so much as a second. "Yes. Do we need a safe word?"

He had a hard time finding his voice after that and all the images it gave him. She was killing him. "No," he managed to grind out. "But I do want you to relax and try not to overthink things. Oh yeah. And keep your hands to yourself. Maybe close your eyes until I tell you to open them too."

Obediently, she squeezed them shut.

And suddenly all that real estate was his to explore. He planned on taking his time.

He glided his palms up her stomach, catching the hem of her top with the backs of his fingers and easing it over her head. He dropped it on the floor at the side of the bed, leaving her in nothing but those skimpy, barely-there panties that left his tongue dry.

He began at the top, cupping the back of her head in his hands, digging his fingers in her tangle of hair while reminding her to keep her eyes closed. He kissed her lids, then her lips. She made a raw, guttural noise of encouragement deep in her throat that spurred him on. He thrust his tongue in her mouth, stroking hers with its edge, and rubbed his erection against the mound of her *mons veneris* until she was squirming and begging for more.

Not yet. He'd only just begun.

He cupped her breasts with his palms and licked first one nipple, then the other, before taking one between his teeth and biting down gently. Her hips shot from the bed.

"Oh, my *God*," she choked out. "Do that again."

She didn't need to ask twice. He tugged with his teeth, again as gently as possible, and licked at the tip with his tongue. He ran his thumbs under the soft swells of her breasts, where they were most sensitive, until she cried out for him to stop. Then, "No, don't. Please. Keep going."

"Babe, tell me what you like. I'll do it."

"I like it all," she said. "Everything you to do to me."

He was so hard now it hurt. Those panties had to come off. He got them as far as her ankles before she kicked them away in impatience.

"I want to touch you," she said. Her eyes remained closed, her hands fisted above her head.

That wasn't a good idea. He had a few more things he wanted to do. "You said you trust me."

"That was before I knew you were trying to kill me."

He laughed softly at that. She wasn't the only one dying right now. He parted her folds with his thumb, then bent his head. She cried out at the first flick of his tongue, her orgasm rippling against him as he talked her through it, crooning encouragement.

"That was the first one," he said, once she stopped shaking. He was on the brink of his own and he was taking her with him.

"I don't think I have the energy for another one."

"I guarantee you do. Remember, you said you trust me."

He eased one of his fingers inside her, then another, lightly exploring the nerves of the clitoris so they could discuss the scientific results for future reference. He worked them in and out. When he didn't think he could wait any longer for her, she started to beg.

"*Now*. Please."

He placed one hand on her abdomen and with the other guided himself inside her. She felt so good—hot, slick, and so snug he was afraid to move, wanting to enjoy the sensation as long as he could. And then he couldn't help it. He thrust, once, twice, then harder and faster. She brought her legs up to encircle his waist, bringing him deeper, and rocked her hips to match the rhythm he set. He clenched his teeth, trying to hang on, but just when he couldn't hold back any longer, he felt the wave of her second orgasm squeezing him tight. His balls clenched in two tight knots, his muscles contracting all the way to his stomach. He shouted out as he came along with her.

Lucky for him he was in good health. That would have been a heart attack otherwise. He dropped next to her, still breathing heavily.

She turned on her side and snuggled against him.

"My day might have gotten off to a bad start, but I've got to say, it ended on a very good note," she whispered.

Her head rested next to his on the pillow, facing him, her full lower lip puckered in a faint, satisfied smile of complete satiation. Pride had him silently pounding his chest. He'd put that look there. He'd love to taste those lips again, and put another smile on them, but he didn't want to wake her.

She lay on her stomach, the sheet pulled up to her hips, exposing the sensual length of her back and the cleft at the flippant round peaks of her bottom. He splayed his fingers across the narrow span of her waist, stroking her skin. Long eyelashes fluttered in her sleep in response, her sweet-scented breath warming his cheek on a soft exhalation.

A wave of pure terror tumbled him head over heels. He loved her. More than he'd ever loved anyone or anything in his life. He was seconds from giving up everything he'd worked for in order to have her. If she opened her eyes now he'd be lost.

And then he'd be ruining two lives, not one.

She could do so much better. She had plans for her future and he wasn't in it. He wasn't going to spend the next few nights trying to make her feel the same way about him. In a few weeks—maybe months—these emotions would pass. Distance would help.

Remaining in her bed would not.

He peeled the bed sheet back and eased out of the bed, gathered his clothes, then tiptoed, naked, across the carpeted floor of the dimly lit room. He eased the door shut behind him. In the spare room at the end of the hall he jerked on jeans and a T-shirt and laced up his shoes. He crammed all his belongings into his suitcase.

Hoping she'd remember him with fondness was the selfish route to take. He left a note for her on the kitchen table: *Dr. Babe. Got called away. Let me know if you're willing to join me in London for a few days while you're in Paris.* He scribbled his number—the one she already had—as an afterthought. The carelessness of it would really enrage her.

Then, with a final look at the closed bedroom door, he walked out of her house and her life.

CHAPTER FIFTEEN

PARIS WAS LOVELY.

Irina flung her briefcase and laptop on the hotel room bed and dropped into a chair by a window overlooking Pont Alexandre. She'd opted to stay in the heart of the city and away from the conference site so she could have her privacy. Her panel presentation was over and she'd had her fill of fielding industry questions for the day, leaving her brain free to disengage, and the life flowing past on the street two floors below her was a welcome distraction.

Three weeks had gone by since Kale slithered out of her bed and her house without a proper good-bye, the emotional coward.

She'd gotten past the hurt stage of loss and moved on to fury. If she closed her eyes she could still read his note with the phone number scrawled across the bottom. Since that number was already programmed into her phone, she knew what the real message was. He'd left it as a pretense that the choice to end things between them was all up to her—the same way he'd turned their last real conversation to fictional children that were nothing more than an excuse for him to ease his conscience about running off on her.

She eyed the phone by the bed, tempted to call room service and hide in her suite for the rest of the evening, but that was too easy. She was in Paris. She should make the most of it. The restaurants down the narrow side streets, away from the tourist attractions, were amazing. She'd brought a cocktail dress she could wear. It was skimpy, expensive, and exactly what Dr. Bev had prescribed. All she had to do was work up the nerve.

But, even if she did, she only had one person she wanted to wear it for. Having the kind of relationship where they saw each other a few times a year strictly for sex might have been something she could have learned to be OK with in the beginning, but now her heart was involved and she'd learned a few more things about pheromones. Once they'd incited a strong physical attraction to one member of the male species, they were hard to redirect. She could write a paper on it.

That made Kale Martin unfinished business. If she planned to move on she had to do something about it.

She drew the curtain across the window and shimmied out of her business suit, dropping the skirt and jacket on the floor. She stared at them for a second, then kicked them aside. She didn't have to go back to the conference tomorrow if she didn't want to. She grabbed a plain white blouse and gray leggings from the foot of her bed. She tugged on a pair of high-heeled ankle boots and reached for her laptop.

Since she was working up nerve she was going to London. She had Kale's number and his phone had a GPS. When she got there, she'd give him a piece of her mind. He didn't get to decide what she wanted. He didn't get to end things between them this way.

She had a say too.

London sucked. It was cold, it was rainy, and if Dan was deliberately setting Kale up for failure he couldn't have lobbed him a better assignment. The usual thrill Kale experienced was gone from the chase.

He'd made such a mistake. Handled things poorly. He wanted Irina more than he did any of this and it was affecting his work. At least he knew she was safe. Dan, despite his complaining, had checked on her for him and made sure the RCMP kept her under unofficial surveillance. CSIS had a presence at the defense conference in Paris so she'd be safe enough there.

There'd been no discernible fallout from the administrative assistant's firing either. Whoever was behind the cyberstalking seemed to have moved on. As for the investment banker… Irina was no doubt the last thing on his mind these days. When Canada's anti-terrorism act had been read to him and he'd learned what the charges against him would be he'd cried like a girl.

A splatter of rain hit Kale's table, creating a dark splash on the wood. A quick glance at the sky warned there could be more where that came from. He was on Broadway Market, not far from London Fields in the borough of Hackney, nursing a mid-afternoon pint between showers at an outdoor pub. Five women in niqabs occupied the table beside him, parcels strewn at their feet as if they'd been up to nothing more than a day of shopping. CSIS, however, suspected they were being used to exchange information by male relatives with terrorist connections. One of the women was a Canadian national bent on making questionable life choices.

Normally Kale enjoyed tailing stupid people, trying to figure out what motivated them, but this situation was beyond his understanding. It wasn't greed or ego driving his target. Her ideology was also in doubt. What sane woman of the twenty-first century gave up her freedom by marrying into a foreign sub-culture noted for its harsh treatment of women? And took on a husband who was the worst of its offenders? How little self-respect must she have?

A lot less than Irina, that was for sure. She knew her self-worth. She'd never forgive him for running out on her. That had been his goal at the time—which made him stupid too and gave him no right to judge other people.

Regardless of this target's poor personal choices the Canadian government continued to claim her as a citizen, and therefore part of a larger problem they had to deal with. CSIS was looking for a name, a date, and a location from her and her friends. That was where Kale and his Arabic came in, but tailing women was always tricky and today was his last chance to get the information. He'd never get this close to her again without tipping her off.

The women, however, weren't cooperating with him. Even though he was doing his best to appear as nothing more than a tourist in need of a break from sightseeing, they'd made it plain they disliked having a strange man sitting so close to them. Any second now they were going to bolt.

"There you are!"

Kale recognized Irina's voice even before turning around. When he did he could scarcely believe it was her. Stalking toward him, all high heels, leggings, and stormy green eyes, was someone who certainly looked like her.

What he couldn't quite get his head around was the spectacle she was currently creating. Irina was the soul of discretion. So, too, was Dr. Glasov, her alter ego. This beautiful, obviously pissed woman was a version of her he'd never before seen.

She slung her bag on a chair and slapped her palm on the table. She leaned forward and got in his face. "You didn't leave me the credit card. How am I supposed to do any shopping?"

His peripheral vision told him the women at the next table were having a good laugh at his expense. Their comments were priceless and made it apparent they had no idea he could understand what was being said. They settled in again, no longer in any hurry to leave and miss the entertainment. Kale was tempted to kiss Irina and add to their fun. The day wasn't going to be a total bust after all.

Instead, he drank in the sight of her. She was cute when she was riled. Hope expanded inside him, nudging the chill of discontent from his soul. Letting her emotions take charge meant there was hope things could be salvaged between them. She wouldn't be here if logic prevailed.

He kicked a chair out so she could sit down. She inched it forward, bringing it close to his, warning him that while she might be playing a part in his current drama her anger was real.

"You showed up at just the right time, Dr. Babe," he whispered to her. "I owe you."

"Don't think for a minute that you and I are on good terms," she replied, her voice equal parts softness and finely-honed steel. "You left without saying good-bye. I deserved better than that."

He had. She did. He reached for her hand across the table, his stomach a mess because of the distinct possibility she might say her piece and leave before he had a chance to say his. She was unpredictable when in a snit and even on a good day he pushed all her buttons. But this wasn't the best time or place to admit he'd made the worst mistake of his life.

"I'm sorry," he said, wrapping his fingers around her tiny palm so she couldn't withdraw. "This is going to make me sound like a jerk but I'm working right now."

"I can see that. So can the whole world." She raised her voice. In the blink of an eye she became whiny and demanding, and so completely unlike her normal self that it threw him. "I'm tired of London. You promised me Paris. I want to see the Louvre, not another stupid soccer game."

"Anything you want, babe."

She could have no idea how heartfelt that declaration was. If she'd give him a second chance he'd do whatever she asked of him. Not right now though. He tried to get his head back in the game, but it was hard. He had a million thoughts running through it that no longer related to work.

Again, this unfamiliar version of Irina saved him. She proceeded to carry on both sides of their conversation, responding to questions and comments he never made so he could listen to what was going on at the next table. Twenty minutes later he had the information he needed.

The five women began gathering their parcels, their discreet meeting over.

Kale leaned across the table and kissed Irina, partly to shut her up, but mostly because he couldn't wait one more second. The faint, fascinating sprinkle of freckles on her nose had been the focus of his attention for the whole time she'd been sitting across from him, babbling on about nothing. He loved the sexy way she clipped her hair up, thinking it made her look professional. He knew from living with her that once she performed her morning makeup routine she rarely touched it again and by midday she always looked as if she'd been having hot sex in a storage closet. That was how she looked now. She was the epitome of the absent-minded professor—although granted, a high-class stripper version.

He'd never wanted her more.

"No one listening to you for the past twenty minutes would ever guess you have a brain in your head," he whispered into her ear.

Her storm-filled eyes remained frosty. "Still angry. And that was the whole point."

"Let's go back to my hotel where we can talk." He stood, taking her hand and pulling her to her feet. He linked their fingers together, not letting go when she tried to tug free. As far as he was concerned she was still a flight risk even though she was the one who'd come looking for him. A punch to the face only took a split second. He knew that from experience.

"Talking is all I came here to do," she warned him. "I have a few things to say to you."

"Understood." He had a few things to say to her too. The last three weeks had been hell. He'd been out of his mind to think he could live without her.

The walk to his hotel took forever. Her heels didn't help up the pace. He thought about hailing a cab but it wasn't that far.

The hotel where he was staying was modern and cheap. He was on the Canadian taxpayers' dime.

Irina scanned the surroundings as they entered the building, no doubt hoping to find a spot on the main floor where they could talk so she wouldn't have to go to his room, but the lobby, while spacious, was open concept and left them nowhere private.

They took the lift to the fifth floor in silence. His room

at the end of the corridor was white-walled and plainly furnished, stark without being drab, the only real attraction a king-sized bed that took up the majority of space. A narrow path cut between the foot of the bed and a desk running the full length of the wall. Generic sheer drapery covered the floor-to-ceiling windows.

He shut the door and threw the deadbolt, then turned to her. Before he jumped on her and swore his undying love or let her ream him a new one, there was one question he'd been dying to ask. "How did you find me?"

"The GPS in your phone."

His eyes almost bugged out of his head. His lower jaw unhinged and swung open. He couldn't believe that Irina, who thought everything to death, would do what she was suggesting, but also didn't see any other way she could have found out where he was. "You hacked into a CSIS phone? Have you lost your mind? Do you understand how much trouble you could be in if anyone finds out?"

She stood beside the bed, her arms folded across her chest, her expression angry and unrepentant. "After I hacked into the RBN for you people? Who's going to report me?"

Not him. Dan either.

But Jesus.

"We do have security on these phones," he felt compelled to remind her.

"If I can hack past it without tripping alarms and it's not even my area of expertise, then you should be more worried about who else might be capable of doing the same thing."

He was impressed and at the same time alarmed. She sounded so practical about committing a federal offense. He'd created a monster. "I'm glad you're on our side." He paused, disconcerted. "You are, aren't you?"

Outside, sheets of cold September rain pelted the window in gusts. She cocked her head to one side. Tendrils of hair too short to be contained by the clip curled at the nape of her slender neck. Her lips pressed into a fine line. "Give me one good reason I should be."

She had every right to be angry with CSIS. They'd used her. But if she was this angry with them, he could only imagine how mad she must be with him. His betrayals were worse. He hadn't told her that CSIS wasn't officially investigating her complaint. He'd hidden the possibility of video footage of their sexcapades from her. He'd talked her into hacking into the RBN when she'd known how dangerous that was, then stood back and let her face the repercussions at work on her own. To top it all off she'd been threatened by someone trying to get back at him.

And then, to really show how upstanding he was, he'd walked out on her in the middle of the night. He'd never considered himself the kind of man who would treat a woman that way, but how would he know? He'd always bailed before things became even close to this serious.

His heart beat too fast for him to catch his breath. She was waiting for an answer and he had no good one to give her as to why she should be on his side at least. Except, perhaps, for one thing.

The tight fist squeezing his lungs eased its grip. He sucked in air, then released it.

"Because I love you," he said.

Those weren't the words she'd expected to hear. And while she wanted to believe them she couldn't. He had no trouble lying—or withholding the truth—to get what he wanted so she didn't dare.

But as she'd walked toward him on Broadway Market and seen he was working, and how poorly it was going, the proof of how stressful his job was had finally hit her. Eavesdropping on people. Lying to them every day…

This whole game of spying was bewildering to her. That didn't mean she couldn't see the necessity for it. She worked in an industry that could endanger whole countries, possibly the world, without some sort of monitoring system. It was why she'd approached CSIS in the first place.

But the very nature of spying created its own breed of problems. Real-world relationships had to be difficult for intelligence officers and any relationship with Kale, if she chose to pursue one, hadn't begun under real-world conditions.

He'd traveled the short distance between the door and the bed and was now in her space, looming over her, almost six and a half feet of pheromone-stimulating male.

"Forgive me if I'm skeptical," she said. "The whole mad dash for freedom in the middle of the night didn't scream warmth of affection to me, let alone love. Since I know you aren't a complete jerk, the takeaway I got from it was terror."

"And you'd be right." He cupped her face with his hands and bent his knees so he could look in her eyes. "You're smart and beautiful. I already knew I wasn't your type. Then I finally figured out you don't need me either. And it hit me that I had too much to lose by sticking around. It was too late for me though. I was already hooked."

She wasn't about to be swayed by a few pretty words from a man who got paid to lie, or be distracted by his sheer male magnificence. She'd made both those mistakes before. More than once. But she understood self-preservation and when his actions were framed in that light it became harder to remember what he'd done that was so wrong.

"Now I've forgotten everything I planned to say to you," she complained.

His hands slid to her shoulders. "Why don't you start with why you're here?"

"I was going to take you up on your offer."

He laughed with genuine amusement. "The hell you were. You're easy to read when you're angry. If I hadn't been working, you would have punched me in the face, then turned around and flown back to France on the next available flight."

"I considered that too," she admitted. "It was going to be one or the other." He was standing so close now, every bone in her body wanted to melt. She was so *easy* where he was concerned.

"To clarify, I was offering an exclusive relationship," he said. "That should have been my first clue that I want a lot more from you than a few days of sex here and there. Not that the sex isn't fantastic," he added, "but I'm after more. And I'm not sure I can give you what you're after."

She refused to feel hope. It was too soon and she wasn't over her anger and hurt. "Why don't you tell me what you think that is."

"Family? Home? Roots?"

"What century did you grow up in?" she asked. "What about me or my career would give you the impression that those things are on my radar right now?" Then the truth struck her. "*You* want those things."

Because he'd never had them. Not in the traditional

sense. With a career diplomat for a father, and now his own work with CSIS, Kale had moved around his whole life.

"Bite your tongue." He, however, appeared as dumbstruck as she was by the possibility.

She started to laugh until tears spilled from her eyes. "*Your* biological clock is the one ticking. Wait until that news breaks on Asgard. Iron Man will love it."

The shock hadn't yet left his face but he managed to recover his sense of humor. "I'm not admitting to any biological clock. And Iron Man would never find out anyway, because he has nothing to do with Asgard. Except for Asgard on Earth, but that's a fairly recent development. We have got to broaden your reading habits, babe."

Typical. He was trying to deflect the conversation from what mattered and turn it into a joke. He wasn't getting off that easy this time. It was going to take more than *I love you* and a funny distraction to make up for the past three weeks of misery she'd suffered.

"If you read one of the textbooks I've written I'll read every one of your comic book suggestions," she said.

"That textbook... Is it first year undergraduate?" he asked, sounding cautiously optimistic.

"No way." She wanted him to suffer. "Fourth year advanced."

He clutched at his heart. "As long as we aren't putting a time frame on this deal, because it sounds like it might take me more than a few days 'here and there' to satisfy you."

"Would you be OK with that?" Irina asked. They seemed to be talking about the same thing, but she was more cautious by nature and had to be sure. "I don't think either one of us should be making any big commitments at this point in our careers. A family, a home… Those things can wait. I'm not ready to work as an independent consultant just yet. You definitely aren't ready for a desk job or being more selective about assignments. Could you be happy with a long distance relationship? And coordinating our vacations so we can spend them together?"

"That right there, babe, is why you're the woman of my dreams." He kissed her, then turned more serious. "All kidding aside, if it makes you happy too, that's all that matters to me. I love you, Irina. I'm blown away by how much. I know you won't believe this but I was ready to quit my job and come find you, only you beat me to it."

"I believe you." She smiled at him, her heart beating ten times too fast. "Based on what I saw today you had something big on your mind. You definitely weren't at the top of your game." Laughter rumbled under his ribs before it erupted above her head in response to her words. "For what it's worth," she added, "I knew I loved you the day I told you our sex life had been caught on tape and you made me laugh about it, then forget how it was all your fault."

"Harsh. Also untrue. I found out about that camera after the fact. We were both victims. But since I stopped paying close attention to your false allegations after you said you loved me, we're good." He wrapped his arms around her and held her tight. "You still angry with me?"

"No." She was as guilty of keeping her feelings to herself as he was. They had a lot to learn about each other and communication was key, so she'd make her position more clear going forward. "But if you run out on me again you're a dead man."

"I wouldn't dare now that I know how easy it is for you to find me." His lips grazed her throat, his hands drifting lower to settle her tighter against him. "This is going to work out, Dr. Babe. I promise."

She believed that too.

EPILOGUE

THEY'D BEEN TOGETHER FOR two years. Five months ago they were married.

Irina was packing for a three week vacation in Barbados. Kale was in the shower, humming a really bad version of a Sam Smith song. They'd decided to make Regina, Saskatchewan their home because her mother's health had declined and her father needed the occasional respite from nursing.

Fortunately Irina's consultancy work kept her as busy as she wanted to be. Right now she'd freed up her schedule because Kale had been away for the better part of two months, and although she'd joined him for a weekend here and there, they were looking forward to spending alone time together without any outside commitments or interruptions. This was to be their delayed honeymoon. Kale wanted to surf. She planned to sit in the sun on the beach and catch up on her comic book reading. He'd kept up his end of their bargain while she was about ten issues behind.

She also had something to tell him and she wasn't sure how he'd take it.

She was pregnant.

They'd decided to stop using precautions and let nature take its course, but neither one had expected nature to be paying such rapt attention. She was happy, and excited, and terrified, all rolled into one pregnant and hormonal package. Kale had an uneasy relationship with his father, she had discovered, which made him nervous about his own abilities in that department. The fault, from what she'd observed, wasn't Kale's. While she liked his family overall, and his youngest brother in particular, his father came across as pompous and entitled sometimes. Fortunately—or not, depending on whether she asked Kale his opinion—her reputation impressed the senior Mr. Martin enough to satisfy him with his son's choice in a wife.

The suitcase was open on the rumpled bed and Irina was standing over it, trying to decide whether to pack bikinis or stick to a one-piece since she wasn't very tall and the baby bump, fast approaching three months, was already noticeable when Kale came up behind her. He nuzzled the side of her neck, cupping her abdomen with his palms. His wet hair, unbound, soaked the collar of her nightie.

"When were you planning to tell me about the baby?" he whispered into her ear. "My birthday? Because that's six months away."

She spun around in his arms. Her eyes widened. "How did you know?"

"After everything we did last night, you think I wouldn't notice the places where you might have—" He stopped and reconsidered whatever words he'd planned to utter. "Changed shape in the past month?"

She ran her palms over his broad, naked chest, her elbows pressed into his rock-solid stomach a few inches above the towel knotted at his hips, her heart beating hard for a couple of reasons. "You OK with it?"

"Have a little more faith in me. I'm a trained observer. I learn from other people's mistakes. I'm already nailing this whole husband gig. The dad part's going to be a piece of cake." He patted her belly with such pride in his eyes it made the baby do twirlies inside her. "This little dude will be rock climbing by his first birthday."

"What if the little dude's a girl?"

"Then she won't be getting out of this house until she's at least thirty-one."

"No double standards I see." Irina kissed his chin, which was all she could reach while in her bare feet. "That's OK. She'll be so busy learning to write code she'll never miss the outdoors." She chewed on the inside of her lip and stared at the base of his throat. "Are you as scared as I am?"

"I'm not at all scared. You shouldn't be either." Kale kissed her, his happiness contagious. "We're an awesome couple. We'll be even more awesome parents. We're going to love this baby until it begs us for a brother or sister to deflect all our attention. This kid won't be able to make a move without us finding out. We've got connections and skills."

Irina sighed with relief. "I'm happy you're happy, but suddenly I'm also a little terrified on this poor child's behalf."

He sobered, turning serious. "I promised when you came to London to find me that things would work out and so far we've been doing just fine. Now I'm going to promise you that a baby is going to make things even better. And if we have more kids down the road imagine how fantastic our lives will become."

Irina had never been much for imagination. Until Kale came along her world had been about technology and scientific data. It amazed her sometimes how much things had changed, not just for her, but him as well. Things were changing again.

And for better, not worse.

NOTE TO READERS

Thank you for choosing *Her Spy to Hold,* the second book in my *Spy Games* series. Kale and Irina were a fun couple to write. And in case anyone is interested, long boarding really has happened on the North Mountain in Nova Scotia. You can find it on YouTube. Crazy kids.

Canada prides itself on its freedom of information policies and public disclosure, and CSIS, Canada's spy agency, isn't exempt. If you read the actual *Canadian Security Intelligence Act*, however, you'll note there's a great deal of ambiguity to their mandate, and my *Spy Games* characters have chosen to exploit it. They are spies, after all.

Next up is Harry and Lies's story in *His Spy at Night*. Her name is actually Marlies because I like it (if we'd had a daughter that would have been her name), but when I shortened it, wow, was that name appropriate. The proper pronunciation is *Lees*, with a soft *s*, by the way, but still…

ABOUT THE AUTHOR

Paula Altenburg lives in rural Nova Scotia, Canada, with her husband and two sons. Once a manager in the aerospace industry, she now enjoys working from home and writing fulltime. Visit her at www.paulaaltenburg.com to view more of her work and to sign up for her newsletter. You can also follow her on Twitter @PaulaAltenburg and friend her on Facebook: https://www.facebook.com/PaulaAltenburgAuthor/.

Read on for an excerpt from *His Spy at Night*, Harry and Lies's story.

Excerpt from

HIS SPY AT NIGHT
HARRY AND LIES'S STORY

by Paula Altenburg

SHE LIKED THAT HARRY was a gentleman throwback to another generation. It set him apart. She enjoyed having him pull out her chair and open doors for her too. Every woman liked being made to feel special. But not when it came to her job.

"This isn't embassy business," she reminded him.

He was undeterred, brushing off her objections as if she hadn't spoken. "We're going back to Plan A. I'm pursuing you. It gives me an excuse to stay close so I can help if you need it."

"I've already got Plan B established. No one at the embassy is going to believe your sudden interest in me."

"No?" The look he gave her made the already small room shrink to a mere postage-stamp size. He tugged at one of her curls, rolling it between his thumb and forefinger. "I'm single and I like beautiful women as much as the next man."

He was playing her own game with her in order to get his own way. While she could hardly complain about the tactics he used she preferred honesty from him. While not completely predictable he was one hundred percent dependable. She trusted him because of it.

And that gave him the advantage, because he certainly did not trust her in return.

All she could do to retaliate was call his bluff.

She stepped in close, placing her hand on his chest. It was solid, like he was, and warm beneath the crisp cotton fabric of his shirt. Her palm prickled with heat. He was only an inch or so taller than she was. If she'd been wearing heels she'd have at least one advantage over him. She met his gaze and read interest. Her breathing quickened, leaving her head spinning. He really did find her attractive. There was an advantage for her in that too.

He had the most beautiful mouth, the lower lip slightly fuller than the top. It was generous and firm, and the color of raspberries in early August. She'd have one little taste. Then he'd call a halt, conceding Plan A was ridiculous.

She pressed her mouth to his, nipping that full lower lip between both of hers and gently tugging. She stroked it with the tip of her tongue. He tasted delicious. Her heart began pounding. A sizzle of heat shot through her belly. Caution kicked up a ruckus inside her head, letting her know in no uncertain terms that she'd made an error in judgment. In this one area he wasn't trustworthy.

Not in the least.

Rather than draw back to neutral territory and regroup, as she should, she threw herself on a landmine. She slid her arms around his neck. His hands came to rest on her back, crushing her breasts to his ribs. A knee nudged her thighs apart. His tongue brushed against hers and her legs threatened to collapse. Harry, far from passive, could kiss.

The coffeemaker coughed, spitting the last of the hot water through the filter to signal the end of its cycle, interrupting the moment. Harry's hands slid down her back to her hips. He lifted his head, his expression as steady and serious as always.

He had nerves of steel.

"I'll introduce you to Vanderloord during intermission," he said, as if the matter were settled. Lies, bemused, couldn't find the right words to argue. He'd proven his point. Her mind was a blank. He eased her aside, his fingers gently biting into her skin before they released her, and slid past her to get to the counter. "You get the coffee. I'll carry the pastries."

She was filling two mugs with the dark, steaming brew before it struck her that this was her home, not his, and they weren't at the embassy pretending he was her boss, and she didn't have to do everything he said.